I, FREDDY

BOOK ONE

IN THE GOLDEN

HAMSTER SAGA

BY Dietlof Reiche

TRANSLATED FROM THE GERMAN BY John Brownjohn

ILLUSTRATED BY Joe Cepeda

SCHOLASTIC INC.

NEW YORK   TORONTO   LONDON   AUCKLAND   SYDNEY
MEXICO CITY   NEW DELHI   HONG KONG   BUENOS AIRES

Text copyright © 1998 by Beltz Verlag, Weinheim und Basel

Programm Anrich, Weinheim

Illustrations copyright © 2003 by Joe Cepeda.

Translation copyright © 2003 by Scholastic Inc.

All rights reserved.

Published by Scholastic Inc., by arrangement with Beltz Verlag, Weinheim und Basel.

SCHOLASTIC and associated logos are trademarks and/or registered

trademarks of Scholastic Inc.

ISBN-13: 978-0-439-28357-1   ISBN-10: 0-439-28357-4

12 11 10 9 8 7 6 5 4 3   8 9 10 11 12/0

Printed in the U.S.A.   23

First Trade paperback printing, April 2005

Text type set in 14-point Perpetua.

Display type set in Johnny Lunchpail.

Book design by Marijka Kostiw

CHaPTER ONE

THE TIME HAS COME.

Enrico and Caruso, the guinea pigs, have settled down at last, old William the tomcat has retired to his blanket for the night, and Mr. John has gone out.

Now is the time to make a start on my life story.

Like any reasonably intelligent writer, of course, I'm wondering if anyone will be interested in what I have to tell. Is my story worth putting down on paper?

I think so. A pretty bright youngster grows up in a kind of prison, is sold, gets shunted back and forth a few times, eventually manages to escape, and is smart enough to gain his freedom. If that isn't a story, what is?

Like any reasonably intelligent writer, of course, I use a computer. Mr. John has given me his password. Nice of him, but quite unnecessary. I cracked his password long ago.

I can crack anything.

Anything, that is to say, from passwords to sunflower

1

seeds and mealworms. Okay, so you don't crack meal-worms, but they're a delicacy we get far too seldom, creatures like us. That's why I mention them here.

MayBE I SHOULD aLSO MENTION I'M a HaMSTER.

More precisely, a golden hamster — in Latin, *Mesocricetus auratus.* Our kind has as much in common with the common field hamster (*Cricetus cricetus*) as, let's say, a modern computer has with an old-fashioned, hand-cranked calculator. We golden hamsters are pretty unique. But more on that later.

No one will turn a somersault in surprise, I guess, if I reveal that my birthplace was a cage. Up to now (or so it seemed!), a golden hamster had no choice but to be born in captivity, while away his little tread-wheel of a life in a cage, and go into Eternal Hibernation there.

The cage containing my native burrow was situated in a pet shop. Great-Grandmother often said we should get down on our paws and give thanks to the patron saint of hamsters for that reason. "Children," she told us youngsters, "in here you get regular meals and a cleaning service as part of the bargain." Great-Grandmother had once been compelled to live in a cage belonging to a girl who, according to her, was as dirty as a guinea pig and as lazy as a neutered tomcat. No regular meals, no cleaning services either. Great-Grandmother very nearly went into Eternal Hibernation before her time.

I'd like at this stage to make something absolutely clear: A hamster's three worst enemies are (a) shortage of food, (b) dirt, and (c) shortage of food. That's why no golden hamster ever passes up a mealworm (unless it smells moldy), nor does he locate his john (for any biology teacher who happens to be reading this along with you: his defecation place) anywhere in the neighborhood of food. Other animals — guinea pigs, for instance — aren't as fussy in this respect.

I was born the sixth in a litter of ten. I shall pass over those first few days of darkness, when all that we blind and naked youngsters did was jostle and scuffle to get at our sources of nourishment — eight of them, if I remember correctly. At any rate, I didn't become a genuine golden hamster until my eyes opened. But unfortunately, my brothers' and sisters' eyes opened too, and then the jostling began in earnest.

I know: Biology teachers call these scuffles "mock trials of strength," and they're supposed to be genetically programmed. Maybe, but I found them irritating. It wasn't that I couldn't hold my own; I simply preferred to think my own thoughts in peace. Believe it or not, I wondered even then why golden hamsters had to live in cages — not that I came to any earth-shattering conclusions.

Until Great-Grandmother took me in hand.

There, and I'd really meant to write about the Golden Hamster Saga at this point. Still, as an author (okay, a budding author), I can imagine that my readers would prefer an action sequence first.

So next I'll describe how I came to be sold.

CHaPTER TWO

SOME TIME BEFORE I WAS SOLD, Great-Grandmother
went into Eternal Hibernation. At first I thought she
was simply taking an unusually long time to wake up.
The pet shop's fat salesclerk knew at once what was
wrong, however, and before I could utter a squeak Great-
Grandmother had disappeared.

I took it hard, unlike the rest of our clan, who barely
noticed. Golden hamsters, as Great-Grandmother had often told me, are loners by nature.

I missed Great-Grandmother. With her I'd been able
to discuss every aspect of golden hamsterdom. When I
tried to do this with my fellow hamsters, my lack of success was spectacular. "Discuss things?" I was told. "Nah, I
just work out. You should try it yourself."

Beat my brains out on the tread-wheel? No thanks,
buddy, not me. Besides, there was only one such contraption in the cage, and the tread-wheel freaks were always

lining up in front of it — or rather, biting and shoving one another aside.

Biting had become all the rage with my fellow hamsters. "Mock trials of strength" were a thing of the past; now, everyone was eager to wage regular "territorial wars," as biology teachers call them. Except that there weren't any territories to fight for; the cage was far too small. Tough luck for the commandos among us, fortunate for the rest, or some of us would have been killed.

The atmosphere in the cage grew worse and worse. We tried to steer clear of one another, but the only way to do that, as we soon discovered, was to hunker down and stay put.

Total apathy set in.

It affected me too.

Sometimes even thinking failed to help. I racked my

brain, but no answers came. My thoughts went around and around in circles . . . until, one day, in the midst of a circle, an idea took shape. The idea grew steadily bigger and more distinct until I finally saw it with crystal clarity: I must get away.

I must get out of the cage.

I MUST FIND a BUYER.

Of course, that was the answer! Why hadn't I thought of it before? Probably because being sold was rather like going into Eternal Hibernation. You simply disappeared, and nobody minded much.

It was clear, at any rate, that the next golden hamster in our cage to be sold must be me. This wouldn't happen of its own accord, though; it would require careful planning. One thing I knew for certain: As soon as the next customer appeared in front of our cage, my beloved brothers and sisters would also reflect on the dreariness of life inside and think it might make a welcome change to be

sold. "Me, me, me!" they would squeak, turning somersaults, leaping into the air, and sprinting away on the tread-wheel, just to draw attention to themselves. When that happened, one particular hamster — yours truly — would catch the customer's eye by doing something altogether different. The only question was, what?

For the first time ever, I took careful note of the television screen mounted high up on the wall in the corner of the shop. It was showing a wildlife video over and over — a lousy, boring film of ornamental fish sluggishly swimming around, brightly colored parrots squawking in treetops, and mountain goats butting one another like maniacs. But there were also some scenes from a zoo. The caged monkeys' behavior shed a very informative light on the relationship between humans and animals. As for the bears in their enclosure, they begged for food in an extremely undignified but highly successful manner. I watched that part of the movie several times, then I was ready. The next hamster buyer could roll in.

Except that he didn't.

It was like a jinx. The demand for golden hamsters seemed to have hit rock bottom. Any number of whistling guinea pigs, squawking parrots, and dumb tortoises were bought and handed over the counter (what do people actually *do* with tortoises?) — indeed, even the Siamese cat found a buyer, when everyone in the store knew she was riddled with worms — but nobody wanted a hamster.

Still, I remained on my toes. Be patient, I told myself. Purely statistically, the probability that someone would come looking for a hamster was becoming greater hour by hour.

And then I nearly overslept.

It was late afternoon — hardly a hamster's most active time of day — and I'd retired to the burrow for a nap. I was roused by loud squeaks, the patter of prancing paws, and the rattle of the tread-wheel rotating at top speed. I awoke with a start and saw at a glance that the time had come.

Or had I already missed the boat?

The fat salesclerk was looking down into the cage, and beside him stood a man with a mustache. I detected a pleasant scent of nutmeg. My fellow hamsters were behaving exactly as I had foreseen. I breathed a sigh of relief; no decision had yet been made. I was just about to go into my routine when I heard the fat salesclerk ask, "How old is your little girl?"

I stopped short.

"She's nearly six," said the man with the mustache.

Too young, far too young!

"Just the right age," said the fat salesclerk.

"The thing is," said the mustache, "I want to teach her a sense of responsibility."

Ah, so she was probably as dirty as a guinea pig and as lazy as a neutered tomcat.

"She spends a lot of time on her own, you see," the mustache went on.

"Great," said the fat salesclerk, "so now she'll have a playmate."

Bad. She'll tote me around all the time.

"Her name's Sophie," said the mustache.

Man, what did *that* have to do with anything?

"And you know what?" the mustache went on. "Although she's only just learning to read, she's asked me to get a book about caring for golden hamsters."

THaT SETTLED iT.

I launched into my routine. While my cagemates were squeaking and turning somersaults, prancing around, and pounding away on the tread-wheel, I darted into the middle of the cage. Then I sat up and begged like those bears in the zoo.

Sit up and beg, and humans will fall for it hook, line, and sinker. Heaven knows what goes on inside their heads. Do they think a hamster on its hind legs looks like a miniature teddy bear or something? Whatever the truth, I stood there straight as a ramrod. Then, I opened my

11

eyes so wide they almost popped out of their sockets. Eyes like little black buttons — how sweet! Mouth slightly open — how fetching! Lips and whiskers twitching — how cute! Oh, look, it's cleaning its little face with its little paws — how utterly adorable!

Well, the mustache pointed me out. "That one looks nice. A little placid though, compared to the others."

I sprang high into the air. Then I performed a second leap, this time adding an aerial somersault (another of the tricks I'd been rehearsing).

The fat salesclerk laughed. "Placid? He's the liveliest one we've got in stock."

The idiot! He'd ruin everything if he wasn't careful.

Sure enough, the mustache turned suspicious. "Are you in a hurry to get rid of him?"

That was it. Quickly, I performed yet another trick I'd been practicing especially hard — I doubt if any golden hamster had ever pulled it off before. Still in the sit-up-and-beg position, I raised my right forepaw as high as it would go, then waved it.

Yes, I waved like those shameless bears.

The mustache laughed. "Okay," he said. "He'll do."

What followed was the worst time of my life, yet it began quite harmlessly, even pleasantly. I was shut up in a fairly small box, but then, hamsters are fond of confined spaces. Next, the box started to move — only a little at first, but soon with such violence that it proved too much for my sense of balance. I was shaken around until I felt thoroughly nauseous. I now know that I was being transported in an automobile. Sick with fear and dismay, all I heard at the time was a nasty humming sound.

At some point — it seemed an eternity later — the humming and shaking ceased. My box was picked up, shaken around some more, and then put down. I heard the mustache call, "Sophie! I've got something for you!"

"What is it, Daddy?"

There it was: The voice of my future mistress.

Me, I couldn't have cared less. It was all I could do to avoid throwing up in my box.

"Here," I heard the mustache say, "see for yourself. But be careful."

"Oh, Daddy! Could it be a . . . ?" Sophie broke off, and the lid of my box was folded back.

There I cowered, flat as a squashed cockroach and blinking at the light like a half-witted chipmunk.

"A golden hamster! Oh, Daddy, he's so cute!"

Save your breath, little girl. I know just how cute I look right now.

"Mom! Look!"

I was still dazzled, but little by little I made out some details. There was the mustache and, standing beside him, Sophie. She was fair-haired and smelled of fresh sunflower seeds. She looked nice and healthy, somehow.

Just the opposite of yours truly!

Then someone else appeared. Also fair-haired, but much taller than Sophie. No smell of fresh sunflower seeds either, just a faint scent of lavender mingled with a hint of tangy chervil.

"Look, Mom! My hamster."

Mom bent over me, and the tangy chervil drowned out the lavender. "Hmm," she said. "He doesn't look too chipper to me. More like he's sick."

Bingo, Mom!

"Gregory, are you sure they didn't pull a fast one on you?"

"Very sure," said the mustache, whose name, it seemed, was Gregory. "He was in great shape at the store."

"Well, he isn't now," said Mom. "And besides, you both know I wasn't crazy about this idea. A creature like this could bring diseases into the house, and that's not a risk I care to take. Gregory, I'm afraid you're going to have to take it back."

"Mom, no!" pleaded Sophie.

"Bring diseases into the house?" said Gregory. "Honestly, Louise! He'll be fine. The trip in the car shook him up a bit, that's all. You should sympathize — you're always feeling carsick."

Bravo, Gregory, give it to her straight!

"That's different," she said. "Okay, have it your way, but if that animal isn't hale and hearty by tomorrow morning at the latest, you'll have to take it back."

"We'll see," was all Gregory said.

Sophie said nothing. Carefully picking me up in the hollow of her hand (she couldn't have done it better), she carried me over to a cage and put me down inside. "There," she said. "Have a nice sleep." She didn't chatter. She didn't try to play with me. She just left me in peace.

YOU'RE a GIRL IN a MILLION, SOPHIE.

Because I was feeling so limp and wretched, I refrained from submitting the cage to an immediate tour of inspection. I found a burrow and curled up in it.

The first thing I wanted to do was to think things over thoroughly, but one thought kept going around in my head: Gregory and Sophie were okay, but Mom — ouch! It was a simple thought, but — as I soon discovered — right on the mark. Then I fell asleep.

CHaPTER THREE

I'M NOW GOING TO TELL YOU about Great-Grandmother. I could claim to be doing so because I've just dreamed about her, or something, but that would be a lie. I'm doing so because this strikes me as the best place for it.

Great-Grandmother often told me, "Stop your nonsense, youngster." She would say this to any young hamster that was horsing around in the cage, but she meant something different every time. She said it to me more than most, and by "nonsense" she meant my everlasting questions. I was a pretty bright kid from the start, as I've already mentioned, and types like me tend to ask questions. What's more, we get far too few answers to suit us.

Fortunately for me, however, Great-Grandmother took me under her wing — if I can put it that way, she being a hamster.

My first brush with her occurred during Saga Hour. Saga Hours are held in every cage inhabited by young hamsters. An old female hamster tells them the Saga, which is something akin to the golden hamsters' Bible. Someone passes it on by word of mouth from generation to generation, and in our cage that someone was Great-Grandmother.

"Now pay attention, all of you!" said Great-Grandmother as she began. She spoke in a hoarse whisper, which made it sound really exciting. We all hunkered down in the litter at the bottom of the cage, cheek by jowl, and listened with hearts pounding and stubby little tails erect.

"In the beginning," said Great-Grandmother, "was the Golden Trinity: three golden hamsters who were abducted from the Promised Land of Assyria and carried off into captivity. And behold, the Golden Trinity swiftly multiplied and developed into a vast race of golden hamsters. And they spread throughout the world so that, today, every golden hamster on earth is descended from the Golden Trinity."

"But, Great-Grandmother," I said, "what about the golden hamsters in the Promised Land of Assyria who *weren't* caught? They must have had babies too, right?" No matter how good the story, I could never turn off my brain completely.

"Stop your nonsense, youngster, and remember this:

THE SAGA IS UNALTERABLE.

You don't question it, you simply listen to it. Understand?"

"Yes," I said, "but —"

"Hold your tongue!" I was alarmed to see that Great-Grandmother had flattened her ears and bared her teeth. Quickly, I started to clean my fur. That's a surefire way of telling an older, stronger hamster you're as harmless as a newborn baby. Although Great-Grandmother eyed me sharply, she seemed to have calmed down.

"And now," she went on, "I'll tell you all what Assyria is like."

The Promised Land had soil in abundance, she said. It was neither too firm nor too loose and contained no stones, so you could dig tunnels to your heart's content without ever coming up against any bars or wire mesh. And the soil was full of earthworms ten times more delicious than the most succulent mealworm. Fragrant fruit and all manner of grain and vegetables grew above ground at every season of the year in such plenty that you could safely do away with the need to hoard them. If you did wish to do so, however, you could dig a storage chamber as big as the pet shop. The quality of the soil in the land of Assyria was so good that this presented absolutely no problem.

I must confess, my mouth started watering and my paws itched and twitched. Even now, however, I couldn't turn off my brain. Why, I wondered, was she making such a song and dance about this Assyria place?

Great-Grandmother described the delights of Assyria awhile longer (for instance, you didn't need a tread-wheel there because you could run straight ahead for days on end). Then she said, "Now, youngsters, pay attention. I'm coming to the point!" Her voice had suddenly changed. She was no longer whispering; her tone was almost exultant.

One wonderful day, she declared, all the golden hamsters in the world would be released from captivity and led back to the Promised Land of Assyria. Then Golden Hamster Liberation Day, which every golden hamster dreamed of, would dawn at last. "Youngsters," said Great-Grandmother, "rejoice!"

And rejoice my fellow hamsters did. They leaped into

the air, squeaking and cavorting. I joined in too, I must admit. For one thing, because I couldn't sit still with all those acrobatics going on; for another, because I was overcome, like the rest, by a strange feeling of elation. But also by the urge to ask a rather awkward question.

The others calmed down and once more seated themselves in silence among the wood shavings, but I found it quite impossible to sit still. The awkward question had somehow lodged in my hindquarters, propelling them to and fro like a hamster's miniature swing.

Then I caught a piercing glance from Great-Grandmother that instantly brought my hindquarters to a standstill.

"Pay attention, all of you!" We were now in the know, she told us. That was not only a great blessing but a duty as well: a duty to yearn for the great day with every fiber of our being — indeed, down to the very tips of our whiskers. Great-Grandmother concluded Saga Hour with the following words: "So hold yourselves permanently in readiness for Golden Hamster Liberation Day. And now, you rascals, you can go off and play."

The other young hamsters trooped off, squeaking and vociferating, to resume their stupid trials of strength.

Me, I continued to sit there defiantly. I refused to be brushed off just like that. Although I couldn't cast doubt on the Saga, I had plenty of other questions to ask. Great-Grandmother looked across at me, then beckoned me over. "Unless I'm much mistaken, youngster, you've got some more questions about the Saga. Awkward questions, I suspect." When I nodded mutely, she said, "All right, out with them."

"But I thought —"

"No, feel free, we're alone now." She smiled. "It never occurs to anyone to question the Saga as a rule, you know, but now and again a thinker comes along, and thinkers have to get it out of their system. So speak."

23

I couldn't afford to miss this opportunity, so I concentrated hard. "First," I said, "I've got a question about Golden Hamster Liberation Day. I can't picture it, somehow. I mean, how could all the golden hamsters in the world flock to Assyria in a single day? How is that possible?"

"No idea."

"Huh? You mean you don't know yourself?"

"Precisely."

"But . . . another thing. Who's going to organize Golden Hamster Liberation Day? I mean, someone'll have to, but who?"

"Search me."

I was flabbergasted. Imagine that! A suspicion took root in my mind. "But the Promised Land of Assyria," I said, "— *that* exists, doesn't it?"

"Not a clue."

"But, Great-Grandmother, what a thing to say! You mean the whole Golden Hamster Saga is just a kind of fairy tale, but I'm still expected to believe in it?"

"Why not? A person can believe in fairy tales." She cleared her throat. "No, to be honest, I'm inclined to disbelieve it myself."

Inclined to? Was the old lady trying to string me along?

"In that case," I said with a touch of boldness, "why sell us this fairy tale of a Saga at all?"

"Listen to me, youngster." Great-Grandmother was deadly earnest now. "Golden hamsters are rather disagreeable creatures by nature. They're crotchety, snappish, and greedy. They hoard food for themselves alone — they'd begrudge their neighbors the rind off a piece of cheese, and sometimes they bite each other to death. I speak from personal experience." She paused for a moment. "They need something to hold them in check. Something to remind them that their neighbors are hamsters like themselves. Something, for example, that every golden hamster believes in: They need the Golden Hamster Saga." She looked at me. "Now do you understand?"

I nodded. Of course I understood. It was quite simple. The Saga was a bite blocker. Great, but somehow less than satisfactory. "And what about this liberation from captivity? I mean, will it really happen someday?"

"Ah, that's just a dream. Anyway, what would be the point? Living conditions inside a cage aren't too bad. Besides, how could it be arranged?"

Where living conditions inside a cage were concerned, I could have reminded her of the girl who was as dirty as a guinea pig and as lazy as a neutered tomcat. But I didn't; I confined myself to her second question.

"If you don't know how to arrange something," I said, "it may mean you haven't given it enough thought."

Great-Grandmother stared at me for quite a while. Then she said, "You're right."

"There must be some way to escape," I said, squaring my shoulders, "and I'm going to find it."

"Now, youngster, stop your . . ." Great-Grandmother smiled suddenly. "If anyone can do it, you can. Don't stop your nonsense, get on with it."

26

CHAPTER FOUR

I WOKE UP IN A BURROW that seemed familiar to me, but my nose issued a Red Alert: unfamiliar smells! I darted out into the open and looked around. I was in a strange cage — and then I remembered: I'd been sold.

I was with Sophie and Gregory — and Mom.

How was I feeling? Terrific. I would show Mom I was in peak condition. That ought to kill off her proposal to take me back to the pet shop.

"Hello, Freddy."

I looked up. Sophie was gazing down at me, fair-haired and smelling of fresh sunflower seeds. But what was this "Freddy" business?

"I thought I'd call you Freddy. You need a name."

Do I? Very well. In that case, why not Freddy? It sounded fresh and frisky, like me. Very appropriate.

"I'll bring you something to eat in a minute. Then you

can make yourself at home. Daddy says I've got to leave you alone until you've settled in."

What a nice, kind, sympathetic family!

"Sophie!" That was Mom from elsewhere in the apartment. "Didn't I say you had to finish your homework before you played with the hamster?"

"Yes, Mom, but Freddy just woke up. I want to feed him, that's all."

"Please do as I ask. That creature can wait."

Some family members were less nice and kind than others, apparently.

"Yes, Mom," said Sophie. Then, in a low voice: "Don't worry, Freddy, I'll bring you something right away."

That was twice Mom had butted in, and she hadn't exactly endeared herself to me the first time. Although I was now hale and hearty, she seemed to have lost interest in my state of health.

So be it. While I was waiting for my food, I could inspect the cage.

"Sophie!"

Mom again. I wondered what was on her mind this time.

"Yes, Mom?"

"I'm getting a migraine. I'm going to lie down in my room for a few hours, and I don't want to be disturbed."

"Yes, Mom."

A door closed.

A migraine? It sounded like something that made you crawl into your burrow for a couple of hours because you didn't feel chipper. I presumed it was the state in which Mom smelled more of lavender than chervil.

Right, now for the cage. Looking around, I saw the inevitable tread-wheel, but also a swing, a jungle gym, and a circular wooden disk that could obviously be rotated. A kind of hamster's carousel? I would try it out later. My future physical fitness had been provided for, anyway. Now for the litter. A brief, experimental dig showed that it was sufficiently firm and deep enough to permit tunneling of various kinds. Next step: Install a john. That was soon done. Now for my burrow. Having wormed my way inside, I discovered that it consisted of three chambers linked by passages. I could use two of them as larders — what more could a hamster want? I wriggled out again and surveyed my new domain.

It all belonged to me.

To me? Yes, to me, Freddy, no one else. There weren't any other golden hamsters around. I was the only golden hamster in the cage!

YIPPIDY-DOO!

I leaped high in the air, turned one somersault, and then — because the first one had worked so well — another.

"There you are," laughed Gregory. "He's himself again, the way I said he would be."

"Too bad Mom didn't see that," said Sophie.

They had walked up to the cage without my hearing them, probably because I was too busy turning somersaults. If wild hamsters fail to hear something, the result — for them — is usually fatal. It's different with us domesticated hamsters; that's why we can practice somersaults.

"Where is Mom, anyway?" asked Gregory.

"Migraine," was all Sophie said.

Gregory's face darkened. He said nothing.

"Daddy, can I let Freddy out? While I do my homework, I mean?"

Let me out? What was that supposed to mean?

"You're calling him Freddy? That's a good name. It suits him, somehow." Gregory grinned. "His full name could be Freddy Auratus. Auratus means 'golden' in Latin."

Freddy Auratus — Freddy the Golden One? No objection. It sounded pretty unique.

Gregory crouched down until his head was level with me. "Shall we let you out, Freddy Auratus?"

Man, will someone explain what it means, all this talk about letting me out?

"Maybe it's too soon," said Gregory, straightening up. "Tell you what: Put the cage on the table —"

Objection! Never move a golden hamster's cage; you could upset the neat piles of goodies in his larder.

"— and open the door. Then he can get out."

Open the door of the cage? So I could simply get out?

Out? But that meant out of the cage!

Yes, that was it! The significance of the words suddenly hit me. They meant nothing more nor less than this: The world was my oyster! I was free! My yearning for release from captivity was beckoning me, Freddy Auratus!

"He can come out if he wants to."

You bet I want to, man, and how!

32

"But if he doesn't, leave him be, okay? If he does go promenading on the table, though, be careful. He could nibble your schoolbooks. . . ."

What gives you that idea, buddy? A Freddy on the loose would have better things to do than nibble schoolbooks, believe me. Like what, for instance? Time would tell. On the other hand, it couldn't hurt to give the matter some thought.

"Or he might fall off the edge and break his neck."

Ouch!

That I could do without. I'd almost forgotten that a life of freedom wasn't without its lurking dangers. What was more, it lacked certain things a cage provided. A safe, snug burrow, for instance, complete with larders. Which reminded me —

"But first I should feed him, Daddy."

a GiRL iN a MiLLiON, as I think I've already said.

The food was a well-balanced mixture of lettuce leaves and grain. The only thing missing was some protein — a mealworm, to cite only one example, but

33

humans seldom if ever think of that. There seems to be an unbridgeable gap between our dietary requirements. I mean, I certainly wouldn't expect humans to grasp how tasty a mealworm can be, but they ought to be taught in kindergarten, if not before, that the little creatures are a valuable source of protein.

Having eaten some of my meal and stowed the rest in one of my larders, I mentally prepared myself for freedom. To do this I settled down comfortably in my burrow and shut my eyes. Then I envisioned an opening in the cage and pictured myself walking through it. I pictured my route to freedom step by step. And where did my last step take me? Back into my comfortable burrow.

I opened my eyes. I had grasped the truth: A closed cage door meant captivity, but an open one didn't signify freedom — far from it. There had to be some route to freedom other than an open cage door, and finding it, I suspected, would be difficult business.

What lay ahead of me was merely an excursion into the world beyond the bars: a pleasure trip during which I

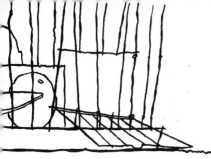

might see something new, but nothing to get worked up about.

I emerged from my burrow.

Sophie picked up the cage, carried it over to the table, and put it down so gently that my meager stores were never in danger for a moment. Then she opened the door. I took no special notice of how she did this — a big mistake, as I discovered later. However, it seemed to be easy enough. I simply saw that the barred door had been folded down at an angle to form a kind of ladder leading to the table.

"Well," said Sophie, "are you coming out?"

What a question! Still, I couldn't help feeling a bit uneasy when I poked my head out. I drew a deep breath. It's only an outing, Freddy, I told myself, so stay cool. Cautiously, I clambered down the bars of the cage door. One little hop onto the tabletop, and I was in the outside world.

I looked back. The cage door — my line of retreat —

was still open. The golden hamster's motto when tunneling: Forge ahead into the darkness by all means, but make sure the route behind you is clear. With this in mind, I began to explore the world beyond the bars.

For a start, because I was anxious to avoid breaking my neck, I tried to spot the edge of the table. No use. Unfortunately, golden hamsters don't have formidably sharp eyesight (in fact, the first person to market golden hamster eyeglasses will make a fortune). So at first I remained within the immediate vicinity. I made out a hardback book, two notebooks, one of them open, and a number of pencils neatly arranged side by side. The table I was standing on seemed to be Sophie's desk. My razor-sharp senses also told me that Sophie had sat down at the desk and was holding one of the pencils in her hand.

A voice in the distance: "I asked not to be disturbed."

Mom again! She made a habit of butting in whenever I was being given food or starting to investigate something.

"Okay, okay, I'm sorry." That was Gregory. "I just wanted to see how you were doing."

"Thanks. You should know by now that these migraines are no fun. If John comes today, please go someplace else to talk. You two are always so noisy."

"For one thing," said Gregory, and you could tell how hard he was trying to keep his voice down, "we're never noisy. For another, we're staying right here. I still have some things to discuss with him before I go on tour, and for that I need my papers, so please . . ."

A door closed. Then silence fell.

Sophie looked up. That was when I became aware that she'd sat there like a statue, hanging her head, while her parents were arguing. She'd looked a bit like one of us when we're scared stiff and play dead. I could sympathize. Young hamsters always find it immensely stressful when two adults fight for territory with their teeth. The contest doesn't end until one of them definitely proves to have the most powerful bite. In this case, considering the way things were between me and Mom, I hoped Gregory would come out on top.

But hamster fights can also have a different outcome, which is that one of the rivals simply gives up and quits the field of battle. Gregory had said something about going on tour. I guessed that meant he would be away for some time. Long enough for Mom to proclaim herself the winner? That remained to be seen. Maybe humans and golden hamsters were different in this respect.

As for the visit by this "John" person, I gave it no further thought. It would have been a waste of time, in any case, because I'd no idea what I was in for. If I *had* known, I would have fled into my burrow like a streak of lightning and plugged the entrance until it was absolutely smell-proof.

So there I sat on Sophie's desk, surrounded by pencils

and schoolbooks, and watched her start on what she'd called her homework. She copied some letters in one of her notebooks, muttering to herself as she did so. The object, it seemed, was to tie up certain groups of letters with certain objects. She did the same thing when she strung groups of letters into words.

I realized, of course, that she was learning to read and write. I knew from my time at the pet shop that written and printed matter was part of a human's life, but it had never interested me. Why should it? Golden hamsters needed no written or printed matter to lead a full life, or so I thought in those days.

At first, though, as I watched Sophie and figured out how writing worked, I merely found it intriguing. You made a few strange marks on paper, and they meant something. For instance, anyone who knew the series of letters for *mealworm* and read them would have a mental picture of one of those yummy little creatures. Fantastic!

Learning to read struck me as far from difficult. In Sophie's schoolbook there were pictures with groups of letters beside them. From the look of it, the T–R–E–E group of letters referred to a picture of a tree. Sure enough, Sophie traced those letters with her finger and said "Tree." So T–R–E–E meant tree.

For experimental purposes, I watched her string together groups of letters and their meanings. No problem — in fact I sometimes worked them out even before she did.

"Sophie?" Gregory had entered the room.

"What is it, Daddy?"

"I have to go out for a bit. If John shows up before I get back, can you give him this list of the points we have to settle? Ask him to get started on them."

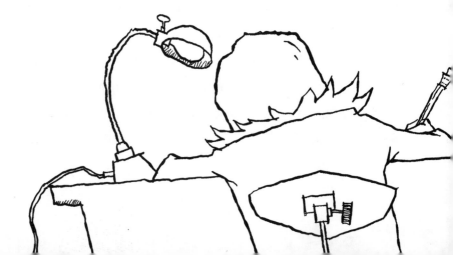

Sophie took the sheet of paper and looked at it. "But I can't read this yet."

"You don't have to. Just give it to him, okay? He'll know what it is."

Sophie nodded and Gregory went out.

As for me, I sat on Sophie's desk with my ears pricked, absolutely transfixed. I was thunderstruck, because I had suddenly grasped why humans use writing and printing: to tell each other things. Gregory wanted to say something to John, but because he wouldn't be there he wrote it down instead. Likewise, if something was printed, it conveyed a message to all who read it. This realization

T-R-E-E =

seems positively silly to me now, as I write these words, but at the time it took my breath away.

Being the kind of individual I am, I promptly pursued this line of thought. It occurred to me how useful the art of reading could be to a golden hamster on the move outside his cage. Not just on Sophie's desk, I mean, but farther away — so far away that it then defied my powers of imagination. What if, in that far-off place, I came across a package that might possibly contain hamster food? If it bore the series of letters that meant "litter," I would know it at once and need not go to the trouble of identifying the contents by gnawing a hole in it. That, incidentally, would also make a noise, and you didn't even have to have the imagination of a mealworm to know that trips outside your cage might present situations in which noise could be dangerous.

So how about it? Was there any reason why not? None, as far as I could see, so I decided

TO LEARN TO READ.

CHAPTER FIVE

I WAS JUST GETTING TO GRIPS with G–R–A–I–N, the group of letters meaning "grain" in Sophie's reader (as her schoolbook was called, I'd since discovered), when a bell rang in the distance. Sophie ran off.

"Mr. John!" I heard her call.

"Hi, kid," said a man's voice.

"Daddy gave me a golden hamster, Mr. John. His name is Freddy. Come on, I'll show him to you."

I was still crouched over the reader, but I sat up and begged. I wanted my mistress to be able to show off a presentable hamster.

Sophie came back into the room followed by Mr. John. He had a big nose, bushy eyebrows, and a leather briefcase clamped beneath his arm.

"This is Freddy," said Sophie.

"Hi, kid," said Mr. John. Was that the limit of the man's vocabulary?

"Well," he went on, "he sure is a hamster and a half."

So he could say other things after all — I even grasped what he meant. It was really funny, what he'd said and the straight-faced way he said it: "He sure is a hamster and a half."

To show the joke wasn't lost on me, I twitched one corner of my mouth and the whiskers that went with it.

"I could swear he understood that," said Mr. John.

Not only funny but smart as well. I took to the man right away.

Mr. John came closer and bent over me. "Hey, little fellow," he said, "twitch the other corner of your mouth."

And that was when the cloud of vapor hit me.

In order to understand my reaction, the reader should know two things. First, a golden hamster's sense of smell is at least as important as his hearing and eyesight, so it's pretty sensitive. Just as our eyes are dazzled by too much light, so our noses are "dazzled," so to speak, when they pick up too powerful a smell, let alone a stench. A stench can be really painful to us.

Second, the golden hamster's many enemies include cats and guinea pigs: cats because they like to eat us, guinea pigs because of their crude behavior and dirty habits. In the pet shop the cats and guinea pigs had been housed a long way from the golden hamster cage. This meant that their smell, although unpleasant, was bearable.

The stench Mr. John gave off, which hit me smack in

the nostrils, was a concentrated blend of tomcat's sweat and guinea pig's pee-pee.

The smell was so strong, it literally knocked me over backward. I was up in a flash, though. I made for the open door of my cage, darted through it, and dove into my burrow. Scraping some wood shavings into a ball, I plugged the entrance with them and lay there, panting hard.

"Oho," I heard Mr. John say, "a contender for the hamster Olympics."

Very funny — sidesplittingly funny. I got up to check if the entrance was airtight, feeling that I wouldn't survive another dose of that stench. This was an exaggeration, of course (and I felt a bit ashamed of panicking like that), but the fact remained: Mr. John and I were through.

"Something must have startled him," said Sophie. "What could it be?"

"I've got a pretty good idea," said Mr. John.

Really? Okay, shoot.

"Hamsters are very sensitive to smells."

Well said, Mr. John.

"Maybe he smelled William on me."

William . . . Nice name, but who did it belong to, the tomcat or the guinea pig?

"Or it could have been Enrico and Caruso, my guinea pigs."

Wow, two of the creatures! No wonder I'd fallen flat.

So William was the tomcat.

Judging by the intensity of the smell, Mr. John must share his home with the animals in question. Why did he torture himself that way? Strange creatures, human beings. At any rate, I was very glad I would never have anything to do with Mr. John's menagerie.

"Sorry, Freddy," I heard Mr. John say, "I didn't mean to scare you."

A real gentleman, Mr. John. Still, the entrance to my burrow would remain plugged for as long as he was on the premises. I treated myself to a little snack and then went to sleep.

I was awakened by Sophie's voice. "You can come out now, Freddy," she called, "Mr. John is gone." Once I'd unplugged the entrance and emerged, she went on, "I'm sorry. The next time he comes I'll tell you beforehand, I promise. And now I'll bring you some fresh food."

At the risk of repeating myself,

SOPHIE WAS a GIRL IN a MILLION.

She kept her promise. The next time Mr. John came, she warned me in advance. She also did this on every subsequent occasion, so I was able to make my burrow airtight in good time. Although not a big job, it was a nuisance — a pity too because I felt sure Mr. John and I would have hit it off together. But there it was: Anyone who consorted with sweaty tomcats and guinea pigs that reeked of stale pee-pee had to forgo the friendship of Freddy Auratus.

Discounting the minor aggravation of Mr. John's visits, I was well off in my new quarters. If I'd had to award grades, my old cage in the pet shop would have earned only an F, whereas as my new cage would have scored an A. Well, a B, let's say, because the menu in a first-class cage includes mealworms, and here, for some unknown reason, I simply didn't get any. However, Gregory did make sure that Sophie kept me supplied with protein in the form of ground beef.

The sports equipment, on the other hand, was state-of-the-art. My favorite apparatus was the circular wooden disk, or hamster carousel. The disk was mounted on its axle at a slight angle, so it turned when you ran on it. Unlike the tread-wheel, which

had made me feel idiotic, it enabled me to run on flat ground, so to speak, with a clear view ahead. I pushed it out into the middle of the cage — quite a strenuous undertaking — and made it my habit to have a good jog every evening.

I would have preferred to run straight ahead, of course. Although Sophie regularly allowed me to romp around on her table, it was too small and cluttered for that. I couldn't get down on the floor either. I ventured to the edge of the table on my second day in the apartment, but what met my eyes was a yawning chasm so deep that I could see no chance of reaching the ground. Climbing down the table leg was out of the question — golden hamsters don't have sticky feet like tree frogs. No, there was only one way of reaching the floor: Sophie would have to put me there.

I tried to make this clear to her by scampering to and fro along the edge of the table and looking meaningfully (or so I hoped) at the floor. But what did she do? She put me back in my cage, clearly convinced that I meant to jump off. (I must say I felt rather hurt that she would think me dumb enough to try jumping without a bungee cord.) After this had happened a few times — even Gregory failed to catch on — I gave up. It all would have been so simple if I'd been able to tell them, "Listen, you guys, I want to get down on the floor." But that was just what I couldn't quite do.

Which brings me to a pretty sore point: the confusingly one-sided nature of our ability to communicate. I mean, I could understand every word uttered by Sophie and other human beings, but the opposite didn't apply. There was almost no way I could make myself understood. True, I was capable of conveying that I was in a good mood (a somersault sufficed), or that I was hungry (I circled my feeding place), or that I was a cute little fellow (I went into my wave-a-paw routine), but that was as far as it went.

This gradually became a problem. An intellectual problem, to be precise.

The fact was, I'd learned to read so quickly, and so

much quicker than Sophie, that I myself was astonished. Maybe a golden hamster's brain is specially designed for reading. (In view of my own intellectual feats, I'm afraid the golden hamster chapters in biology books will have to be rewritten someday.) Whatever the truth, I could read quite fluently quite soon.

And then I became hungry — hungry for reading matter.

But I didn't get any.

The only book on Sophie's desk was her reader, which was always open at the pages she happened to be working on. All they showed were pictures of things with the relevant words beside them, or sometimes short sentences, but nothing that would satisfy my hunger for real reading matter. I tried once or twice to open the book at pages nearer the end, where I guessed there was some more advanced and interesting stuff, but all that happened each time was that Sophie put me back in my cage. She was probably afraid I meant to nibble the paper. She had no inkling that I was Freddy Auratus, the remarkable hamster

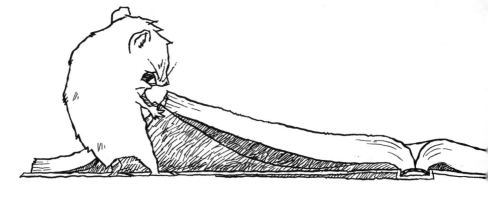

who had learned to read and was hungry for mental stim-
ulation. And I couldn't tell her so.

I thought of writing to her, naturally, but how? With a
felt pen? We hamsters can do plenty of things with our
paws — excavate an elaborate system of tunnels, for
instance — but we can't, unfortunately, wield a heavy
writing implement well enough to produce something
readable. And even if I *had* managed to scrawl something
that resembled letters, Sophie still would have failed to
see them as letters. Why? Simply because she would have
found it impossible to imagine my having written them.

I might have been able to convey to someone as smart
as Mr. John that a hamster was trying to get in touch with
him, but that was out of the question for obvious reasons.

Gregory was another possibility, but he was seldom at

home. I'd discovered that he played the trumpet in an orchestra. I got a terrible fright when I first learned that, wondering how I would protect my hypersensitive ears. Fortunately, he never practiced on the premises.

And Mom? Trying to establish contact with her, even if I'd wanted to, would have been as futile as chatting with the moon. I never saw her. She never paid a single visit to the cage, not even to see if I'd recovered from my car-sickness.

For my part, I could have happily dispensed with Mom's attentions. I'd like to be able to say that I didn't exist as far as she was concerned — that she ignored me altogether.

But it wasn't so.

Unfortunately for me, she was achingly aware of my presence.

CHaPTER SiX

"SOPHIE?"

"Yes, Mom?"

"Bring me a glass of water, would you?"

It was lunchtime, and although our kind likes to sleep until nightfall, I'd left my burrow because Sophie had just come home from school and was going to feed me. And now Mom had butted in yet again — from her bedroom. I don't know how she managed to hit on the crucial moment at such long range. Some kind of mysterious telepathic powers, I guess.

"Right away, Mom. I'll just feed Freddy first."

I'd have bet my entire hoard of food on what would come next.

"That creature can wait."

BiNGo. Plus a special bonus for predicting her exact words.

"I have to take my pills."

"Yes, Mom." Sophie disappeared, leaving me empty-pawed.

Okay, so it wasn't an absolute tragedy — I would get my food in due time — but I was annoyed. For one thing, by Sophie's eternal, dutiful "Yes, Mom." Okay, okay, she naturally couldn't tell Mom to fetch her own glass of water, but in her place I'd have talked back occasionally. Just a little, at least.

But maybe I was looking at it the wrong way. Maybe Sophie *enjoyed* fetching Mom glasses of water, not to mention all the other things demanded of her.

Because Mom made Sophie jump to it quite often. Sometimes she'd be sent to fetch an extra pillow, or an extra blanket, or a damp cloth (for Mom's

forehead), or a Walkman (when Mom felt like some music during her migraine). I'm not saying Mom could have fetched all these things herself. She probably couldn't help getting her migraines in the afternoons, when Sophie was home. All this I'm prepared to admit was true.

But one thing really *was* unnecessary, and that was my second source of annoyance: the fact that Mom always called Sophie just when she was feeding me.

"Here you are, Mom." Sophie, far away in Mom's bedroom, must have brought her the water.

"Thanks." I could hear Mom drinking. Then she said, "You're always messing around with that animal when I call you."

"But I've got to feed him."

"Yes, I know, but remember this: Hamsters are solitary creatures. If they aren't left in peace they get stressed."

True. Thanks for the kind thought, Mom, except that it didn't apply to Sophie. Sophie looked after me and left me in peace, just like I needed. Anyway, why this sudden concern for me on Mom's part? Then I grasped the truth.

She wasn't worried about my well-being at all. It was about Sophie. Mom couldn't bear Sophie looking after me; that was why she butted in whenever I was being fed. It came to me in a flash: Mom wanted Sophie all to herself.

How ridiculous. Me, a tiny golden hamster, a rival for Sophie's affections? Was Mom really afraid I'd take her place? I mean, she wasn't a newborn hamster to be shoved aside by fellow competitors for their mother's milk. Clearly, something was going on inside her that our kind couldn't understand. Whatever it was, I felt as if I'd picked up an unfamiliar scent. Warning lights flashed in my brain: Mom was a potential danger!

But what kind of danger? The possibility that she might insist on returning me to the pet shop had been banished for good, I reckoned, now that I was in such great shape, and I couldn't think of anything else. At all times, I would have to be on my guard.

I started to think up some precautions. Against what, though? Because I didn't know, this promised to be a pretty futile occupation. Then Sophie came back. Mom had gotten what she wanted, so now I could be fed. Sophie actually managed to give me my food without further interruption. Then she carried my cage over to the table, opened the little door, and I clambered out. I'd only just sat down beside the reader when a voice called in the distance.

"Sophie?"

"Yes, Mom?"

She really had the patience of an angel, that girl. Careful, though! Maybe Mom was getting ready to strike the first blow against me.

"Bring me some tissues, would you?"

Maybe not.

"Yes, Mom." Sophie got up and walked to the door. She was actually going to leave the room — leave me sitting on the table all by myself.

At last! I would be alone with the reader at last! Now I could leaf through the pages in peace and look for something really interesting to read.

But then Sophie stopped short and swung around. Returning to the table, she picked me up and put me back in my cage. The little door shut with a click. Then she left the room.

Me, I sat slumped behind the bars. Disappointed at first, then more and more exasperated. I got really mad at Sophie. Out of my cage, into my cage, just as her ladyship pleased — as if I were an inanimate object. It didn't occur to her that an animal like me was a living creature whose wishes might extend to something more than an adequate diet and a clean cage. But if Mom so much as sighed, she came running. Humans be darned! Good riddance to the whole bunch! Independence was what I needed. Out of my cage, into my cage — yes, but just as *I* pleased. Why not? Why shouldn't I open the cage door myself? That would certainly be a useful precaution against any future skulduggery on Mom's part. If danger threatened I would simply vanish, leaving Mom high and dry. So there!

I climbed up the door and inspected the fastener at the top. An absurdly simple mechanism: The bar above the door curved down in the center to form a flexible catch that snapped into place when the door was shut. To open it, all one had to do was climb up and apply outward pressure. It was positively primitive!

But highly effective. Strain as I might, and no matter how hard I braced my nose against the catch, I wasn't strong enough to disengage it. I gave up, at least for the moment, and climbed down again.

I had to do so in any case, because Sophie came back into the room. She couldn't be allowed to suspect, not at this stage, that I was debating how to open the door of my cage. Exactly how, time alone would tell.

"Here, Freddy. Something tasty for you." It was an extra ration of ground beef.

SOPHIE WAS a GIRL IN a MILLION after all, and one who, compared

to me, must possess the strength of an elephant. When she opened the cage door again, she simply disengaged the catch by pressing it down with her thumb. How would *I* ever manage that?

"Sophie?"

"Yes, Mom?"

"Have you seen my glasses anywhere?"

It was evening now. Sophie had put me back in the cage and Mom seemed to be over her migraine for the day.

"Yes, Mom. They're on the sofa in the living room. Beside your book."

Beside Mom's book? Did that mean Mom also had some books?

But of course, why hadn't I thought of that? Of course Mom read books whenever she didn't have a migraine. She didn't sit watching television (that I would have heard), so she must have a hoard of reading matter someplace. Instead of hoping to find something readable on Sophie's desk someday, I ought to figure out how to get at Mom's

store of books. That would solve my problem in a flash —
my intellectual problem, I mean.

The problem of how to get the cage door open showed
no signs of resolving itself. I would simply have to
devise some method or other. Hard as I racked my brain,
however, absolutely nothing occurred to me. In order to
relax, and because it was the right time of night for it,
I went jogging.

The moment I climbed onto the carousel and the
angled wooden disk revolved a little under my weight —
at that very moment, I saw the light. I suddenly knew how
to open the cage door.

But only in principle, because I had to rack my brain
some more before I figured it out in practice. One thing
was obvious: I needed a fairly long lever so that I could
insert one end beneath the door catch. If I hung on to
the other end with all my might (possibly increasing my
weight by the addition of two well-filled cheek pouches),
the catch would be bound to spring open.

But where to find a suitable lever?

That problem too I solved in less than a minute. In theory, that's to say, because in practice I was regrettably obliged to wait until the afternoon of the following day. To an enterprising golden hamster with great plans in mind, that seemed an awfully long time. I couldn't even use the delay to work out what I would do if I actually got the cage door open. Everything would depend on whether I could reach the floor. And that was doubtful, because my cage usually stood on a shelf against the wall. Although the shelf was low, there was no way of climbing down as far as I could see — but only as far as I could see with my rather poor eyesight. The shelf seemed to be a long one. What awaited me at the other end?

I flitted nervously to and fro inside my cage like a swallow before a thunderstorm. The ensuing night tried my patience to the limit.

But morning came around once more, then lunchtime, and then, at long last, the waiting was over. Sophie returned from school and fed me (Mom didn't butt in for once, strangely enough). Soon she would start on her homework. That meant she would put my cage on the table and I would be able to solve my lever problem.

But she didn't do any homework.

She didn't stay in her room either. She spent the time elsewhere in the apartment. I could hear her walking around — restlessly, somehow. Gregory was also on the move a lot. It seemed he was getting his things together, articles of clothing for the most part. Once I heard him ask Mom where his white tuxedo could have gone, to which she shot back that she wasn't his maid. Mom had been spared a migraine today, incidentally, but was also in the grip of some restless urge to move around. What the heck was going on?

The commotion in the apartment persisted through-out the afternoon, and I simply couldn't make heads or tails of it. Then the doorbell rang.

"Gregory, your taxi's here!"

"Coming!" Gregory called. Then I heard him tell Sophie, "I'll try to call you every couple of days, okay? I'll only be gone two weeks this time."

Then I got it: Gregory was going away! Of course, he must be going on tour with the orchestra.

And Sophie and I were staying behind on our own.

On our own with Mom.

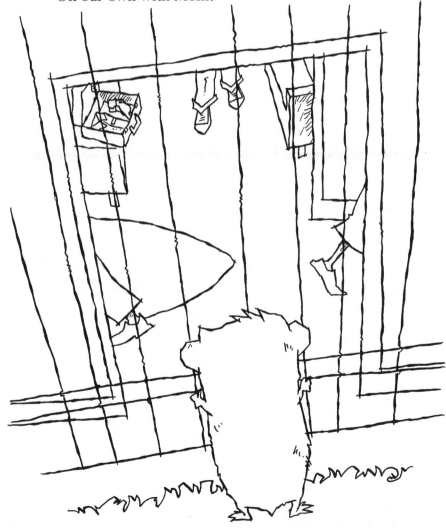

CHAPTER SEVEN

I CRINGED WITH FEAR AT THE THOUGHT. Mom had a free hand now. She could do what she liked with me — anything that came into her head.

Panic, sheer panic, overcame me. With effort, I managed to pull myself together sufficiently not to bite the bars of my cage like a demented skunk. I darted into the burrow and started rearranging my larders. It was high time I did this in any case, and it would probably calm me down.

But it wasn't until I'd shifted every morsel of apple, every lettuce leaf and sunflower seed, from one larder to the other at least three times that my brain regained its power of thought — more or less. Okay, I said to myself, now figure out what Mom is likely to do.

She would take me back to the pet shop, of course.

But only if I wasn't in peak condition.

Right. Except that that had been Mom's pretext while

Gregory was around, and now she didn't need it anymore. She could get rid of me for no reason at all.

And Sophie? She would naturally want to keep me, but Mom would overrule her without blinking an eyelid — that much was distressingly obvious. No, Sophie couldn't help me. I would have to help myself.

That was why the next item on my agenda was

"OPERATION OPEN DOOR."

I was able to make a start on it the same evening.

Sophie had supper with Mom, then came into the bedroom and tipped out her backpack. Of course, she hadn't done any homework yet.

I rose on my hind legs, gripping the cage door, and Sophie caught on at once. "Want to come out?" she asked. "Of course you can." She carried the cage over to the table, put it down with her usual care, and opened the door.

It had struck me that the best plan would be to make for my objective right away. If Sophie didn't play along at once, I would still have time for several more attempts. She would have to cooperate, that was clear. I couldn't possibly transport the thing into my cage in secret — behind her back, so to speak.

I climbed out and scurried across the table. There the pencil lay, long and thin and better suited for use as a lever than all the other pencils and pens. I gripped the blunt end in my teeth so that, by turning my head sideways, I would be able to maneuver it through the cage door.

"No, Freddy!"

Okay, not this time. I let go of the pencil and Sophie put it back. I waited a while, then started again from scratch.

"No, Freddy, I need that."

So do I. A lot more than you do, in fact.

The next time I hung on to the pencil a bit longer. Sophie sighed when I finally let go and she put it back in its place.

I sighed too, inwardly. It seemed to be developing into a battle of wills. Okay, try again.

"No, Freddy! You can't have it!"

"Sophie?"

Mom, outside the door. I was so startled, I dropped the pencil. I pulled myself together at once and made another grab for it, but Sophie was too quick for me.

"Yes, Mom?"

"Is that the hamster you're talking to?"

Congratulations, Mom. Really astute of you.

"Yes, he's playing with my pencil."

"You mean that creature isn't in its cage?"

A brilliant deduction. All she had to do was look in, but it obviously hadn't occurred to her.

"He's only on the table, he can't get down."

"Still, please lock him up in his cage. And right now."

Darn, she's ruined it!

"But why, Mom?"

"Please do as I say, Sophie!"

"Yes, Mom."

"And Sophie, that creature stays locked up from now on. We don't want it escaping and hiding somewhere in the apartment. Have I made myself clear?"

"Yes, Mom."

There it was, Mom's first attack on me. She marched off down the hall, and her footsteps sounded firm and self-satisfied.

My only remaining hope lay in swift and decisive action. Sophie was still holding the pencil. I bounded over to her and sank my teeth into it. I bit it so hard I was scared it would snap, but I had to take the chance. Now that the thing was between my teeth, it felt like it had always been there.

Surprise had made Sophie let go, but she grabbed the pencil again and tugged. "Give it, Freddy!"

NO WAY. I screwed up my eyes and flattened my ears.

Sophie continued to tug and shake the pencil like a dog worrying a bone. "Freddy! Let go!"

Not on your life. I hung on doggedly and let her shake me to and fro. Didn't she understand?

"Okay." She let go at last. "I'll give it to you as a present. You can take it into the cage with you."

As I think I've mentioned more than once, she was **a GiRL iN a MiLLiON.**

It was midnight before I could finally set to work. Until then, Sophie had kept tossing and turning restlessly in her bed. Now she was lying still and breathing deeply. She was obviously fast asleep, so I could risk making a bit of noise. That was unavoidable, unfortunately. I looked forward to my attempt to open the cage door with rather mixed feelings, aware that all kinds of things could go wrong.

But nothing did.

I'd like to be able to report that opening the cage door was an extremely difficult, dangerous, nerve-racking operation. The truth is, it was a breeze.

Using my carousel as a platform, I inserted the tip of the pencil under the spring catch at the top of the door and applied my weight to the other end. There was a faint click, and the door opened. It didn't even topple outward, so I was able to fold it down without a sound.

It had all been so easy, so childishly simple, that I was rather disconcerted and crouched on the open cage door for several seconds. It took me another few seconds to realize something: **I WaS FREE.**

Really free, this time. No one had let me out; I had freed myself by my own efforts.

I suddenly felt so light I could have soared into the air. At the same time, my fur felt so thin that the faintest breath of air made me shiver.

I shook myself! No weakness, not now! Cautiously, I made my way along the shelf to the end I'd never been able to see before. Luck was with me: The shelf ended beside a window, and the curtain reached down to the floor.

Things got rather exciting — for a hamster, at least — once I'd climbed down there, because the smells that assailed me were almost as powerful as those given off by Mr. John. One of them was pee-pee — dog piddle, probably. Sophie must have brought it home among the many scents on her shoes. My nose soon became positively numb with them, so I had to rely on my ears when exploring further.

Having since become something of an expert on human beings, I guess I'm qualified to state that none of them has a clue how accurately golden hamsters can pick out sounds and identify them. For instance, even if a violent thunderstorm is raging, we can hear a mealworm wriggling someplace. Okay, so I'm exaggerating. But not a lot.

What I mean to say is, it was child's play for me to locate Mom's breathing.

74

And because it was customary in this household to leave all the doors open, at least a crack (I knew this because of our legendary sense of hearing), I very soon had the pleasure of sitting beside Mom's bed.

It was, if I may put it this way, a rather exciting situation.

However, I resisted the urge to do something rash — like nibble Mom's nose, for instance. Instead, I concentrated on my real reason for being there: I wanted to get at her reading matter.

But I failed to find any.

I darted to and fro in search of a stack of books, but in vain. Then I chanced to look up, and in the glow from the streetlight outside the window I saw them. Mom kept her books high up on the wall. I made out a whole series of shelves, one above the other, and all of them held books — countless books.

I had discovered a literary treasure house.

My intellectual problem was solved. How to get at the books on the shelves was something to be figured out on my next excursion. I had achieved enough for one night.

Feeling satisfied, I returned to Sophie's room and got back into my cage. And that was when I did, after all, encounter a minor problem. In order to shut the door (not even Sophie must be allowed to know that I could open it) I had to maneuver it back into place so the catch engaged, once more using the pencil as a lever and the carousel as a platform. It took some doing, and if hamsters sweated — which they don't — my fur would have been soaked by the time I was through.

When the job was finally done, I buried the pencil beneath some wood shavings (I didn't want Sophie deciding to take it back) and curled up in my burrow. Although it was the middle of the night, and I should really have been chirpy as a cricket, I was feeling sleepy — probably because I'd canceled my mental Red Alert.

The situation had eased. I could now exit my cage and hide someplace safe at a moment's notice. All my problems were under control.

The Mom problem in particular.

Or so I thought.

CHAPTER EIGHT

HAVING GONE TO SLEEP in the middle of the night, I was much livelier than usual when morning came. It was eight o'clock, and Sophie was still in bed. I was debating whether to have an early morning workout when the bedroom door opened.

Mom appeared.

Maybe this was normal — maybe Mom came to wake Sophie every morning while I was still asleep. What was *abnormal*, I was pretty certain, was the way she looked today.

Her face was all swollen up and the color of a tomato.

"Sophie," she said in an icy voice, "wake up."

"Huh?" Sophie stretched and blinked. She seemed surprised to find Mom beside her bed. Then she sat up with a start. "Mom! What's the matter with you?"

"An allergic reaction."

"A what?"

"A kind of illness caused by an irritant."

"An irritant? What's that, Mom?"

"It can be any number of things. The chemicals in a detergent, for instance. Or cat hairs."

Cat hairs? I literally froze with fear.

Sophie still hadn't caught on. "But we don't have a cat."

"Not a cat," said Mom, "but a hamster."

"Freddy, you mean?" Sophie's eyes widened. She hadn't a clue what all this was leading up to.

Secretly, I crept toward the entrance to my burrow. Better to do a disappearing act, I thought, though I doubted that would help. Nothing but the Hamster God's personal intervention could save me now. Just as I slipped into my burrow I saw Sophie stiffen.

"But . . . you don't mean Freddy!"

"I'm sorry, but I'm afraid the hairs from his fur are making me ill."

Like heck she was sorry, **THE CRAFTY SKUNK!**

"But, but . . ." Sophie stammered. Then agitation sharpened her wits. "Look, Mom, Freddy's been here a while now, and you've never had an — well, you've never had one before."

"An allergic reaction. True, but why not? For one thing, because I've been careful not to go near him; for another, because his hairs have taken this long to spread around the apartment. In short —"

"But, Mom!" A note of despair came into Sophie's voice. "It could be something different. Why are you blaming Freddy?"

"Because I know it," Mom said coldly. "Anyway, it's obvious what we have to do now."

"What?" Sophie still refused to understand.

"Really, Sophie, you know as well as I do."

"No, Mom! No!" Sophie started to sob. "Please don't!"

"Come on, Sophie, you think I'm enjoying this? Look at me. You can't want your mother going around in this condition. And, I'm running a fever."

"But it doesn't mean that Freddy —"

"You bring him into our home and I get an allergy, what more proof do you want? That creature is going —

79

this morning. We're taking it back to the pet shop. I'm sorry, but there it is."

I heard Mom leave the room. Sophie was sobbing loudly now. I mean, we hamsters aren't prone to sentimentality, but it really got me down to hear her. I crawled out of my burrow. Sophie was standing beside the cage in her nightie, gazing at me with tears trickling down her cheeks.

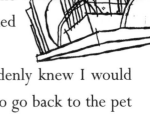

I hadn't realized she was quite so attached to me.

As for me, I suddenly knew I would miss her — *if* I had to go back to the pet shop.

But I didn't have to. Why not? Because I would escape from my cage first. I was determined to go into hiding.

My chances were pretty good. The apartment was large, with lots of pieces

of furniture to hide under. Above all, though, it was part of an old building, so there were any number of cracks, gaps, crevices, and holes into which I could vanish without a trace. What about food? It would be bad luck indeed if I couldn't find some in the kitchen or elsewhere. No point in kidding myself, though: Life would be hard. But leave this place? Leave Sophie and go back to prison in the pet shop? **NEVER!**

If only Sophie would stop looking at me! I couldn't open the door unless she did. It would be better if she couldn't gaze at me so intently. I crawled back into my burrow, and sure enough, a little while later I heard her leave the room as if she'd come to a decision.

Now!

Quickly, I dug out the pencil and lugged it over to the carousel, listening for sounds outside the room. I couldn't afford to let Sophie catch me unaware. After all, she wasn't in on my plans. She'd be bound to take away my lever, and that would ruin everything.

Sophie was talking to Mom in the kitchen. I could only

hear snatches of the conversation, but she was obviously trying to talk her out of it. A waste of time, naturally. Just as I was climbing onto the carousel with the pencil in my paws, I heard Mom say, "Right, I'm going to call John."

Mr. John? Why would she call him?

Of course, she needed him to take me back to the pet shop. Except that Freddy Auratus wouldn't be around when he showed up. I proceeded to maneuver the tip of the pencil under the catch.

Just then, Sophie came sprinting along the passage at a rate I wouldn't have thought her capable of. I jumped off the carousel and buried the pencil in double-quick time. I had just started cleaning my whiskers, all innocent-looking, when she burst into the room.

"Freddy!" she cried. "What if . . ." She broke off and eyed me thoughtfully. Strange, what had she been going to say?

She sat down on her chair — sat there rooted to the spot, gazing at me. I was on pins and needles. We waited. Then the doorbell rang and she raced off again. I promptly began to dig up my pencil again.

"Mr. John!" I heard Sophie call.

"Hi, kid."

I climbed onto the carousel, but I could already hear them coming down the hall, so I hastily reburied the pencil. A moment later Sophie came into the room followed by Mr. John: bushy eyebrows, big nose, and the seemingly inevitable leather briefcase under his arm.

"Hi, kid." My first impression was confirmed — Mr. John seemed like a really nice guy. He was considerate enough to remain standing in the doorway, so the smell was just bearable.

"Well, Sophie," he said. "I'll do it for your sake, but I don't think he'll like it."

I was transported in my cage, not the box I'd arrived in. At least I would be able to survive the journey in a smell-proof burrow — an important consideration, because Mr. John came too close for comfort when carrying the cage out of the apartment. Sophie came too, which soothed my nerves a little.

Mom I never saw again. That much, at least, I was spared.

From the sound of his footsteps, Mr. John carried the

cage down some stairs. Then a door opened and I was instantly bombarded with noise, a harsh mixture of sounds ranging from the highest to the lowest frequencies. I crept deep into my burrow, feeling utterly miserable. So this was the end.

Good-bye to a cage of my own!

Good-bye to reading books!

Good-bye, Sophie!

Golden hamsters can't weep. If things prove too much for us, we sink into a state of apathy. Our love of life is extinguished. We even lose interest in food. At that moment, not even ten mealworms would have coaxed me out of my burrow. My heart was as heavy as lead.

At some stage I heard a door open. Then it closed and the noise died away. We had reached the pet shop. So that was that.

Hey, what was happening? The pet shop was all on one level, but my cage was being carried up some stairs — some pretty steep ones. What was going on? Where on earth were we?

Mr. John and Sophie came to a halt. A handle turned and a door creaked open. Mr. John's mixture of smells grew suddenly stronger — quite a bit stronger. I could tell this even inside my burrow. Phew, what a stench! Before long my nose was as numb and insensitive as a human's. I heard the door close. Mr. John carried my cage for another few steps, then put it down.

"Well," he said, "this is as good a place as any, I guess. He's far enough from the other two in here."

What other two?

"But he'll have to stay in his cage, I'm afraid," Mr. John went on. "It's too risky."

Too risky? What was he talking about?

"William's a lazy old thing, I know, but I can't be sure about him."

WILLIAM? William, the sweaty tomcat?

I caught on at last.

I was at Mr. John's place. I'd wound up with Mr. John and his menagerie.

CHAPTER NINE

IF IT'S TRUE THAT FEAR STRESSES you out, and that stress shortens a golden hamster's life, I had just grown older in pretty short order. I made a desperate attempt to assess my situation, but with absolutely no success. The same thought — I'm at Mr. John's place, I'm with Mr. John and his menagerie! — went around and around in my head until I finally told myself: Wait and see. Don't drive yourself nuts; just wait and see what happens. I felt a little better after that.

Not that this disposed of the smell problem. There was no getting away from it. Although the entrance to my cozy burrow was plugged, the air reeked of (a) cheesy tomcat's sweat, and (b) acrid guinea pig's pee-pee. In human terms, it was like being cooped up in a bedroom with a vat of liquid manure. I breathed as shallowly as I could.

"Freddy!" That was Sophie's voice. "Come out, I've brought you some food."

Come out? The air was probably sulfur yellow with the stench. No, thank you! Besides, I had some food in my larders — not that it would last me very long.

"Give him time," said Mr. John. "He'll have to get used to the smell first. It won't be easy for him."

Very tactful of you yet again, Mr. John. Get used to it, though? Never!

"Freddy!" Sophie wasn't giving up. "There's some food here, Freddy."

"Well, kid," said Mr. John, "it's time for school, but you can pay him a visit this afternoon."

"Okay, Mr. John." Sophie sounded sad. "But what if Mom won't let me come back?"

What about tomorrow? What about the future? This might be my very last opportunity to lay eyes on Sophie. I drew a deep breath, removed the ball of wood shavings plugging the entrance to my burrow, and crawled out.

"Freddy!" Sophie's face lit up. "Look, Mr. John, he's fine."

Absolutely fine, as long as I held my breath. Heck, I

had to breathe in already! If Sophie hadn't been there, I would have high-tailed it back into my burrow. But I managed to stick around. And what can I say? After a while the smell became just bearable.

"Welcome, Freddy," said Mr. John. "This is your new home."

Hmm . . . Five minutes ago I'd have thought: Better the pet shop than this dump. Now I wasn't so sure.

"Here, Freddy," Sophie tipped the contents of a paper bag onto my feeding place. "See what I brought you?" It was an assortment of all the things I liked best — a big enough assortment to console me for whatever tribulations I might still have to undergo.

Permit me to say it one last time:

Sophie was a girl in a million.

Once Sophie had gone and I'd stowed the food away in my larders, I tried to form an idea of my new home. First, the smells. These informed me that the tomcat and the two guinea pigs must be housed in the room next door, where Mr. John had gone after leaving me.

Then the sounds. These made a rather vague impression. The deep breathing I could hear was undoubtedly Mr. John's. He sounded as if he were asleep. But now, in the morning? Very exceptional for a human. There was also a low hum, or more of a faint purring sound, that rather puzzled me. Could that be the guinea pigs? Then came a sudden, high-pitched whistle — no, two whistles: a series of notes or kind of melody resembling a duet. It was awful but unmistakable. Only Enrico and Caruso, the guinea pigs, could have made it. Which meant that the purring came from William. I had no idea a tomcat was capable of making such a pleasant sound.

Finally, I used my eyes. Looking around, I saw that my cage was situated on a shelf. Also on the shelf, to the left and right of it, were books. My cage was in the midst of books — I was on a bookshelf!

Where reading matter was concerned, I had wound up in the land of milk and honey, and my pencil-lever was the passport to it, so to speak. I sighed with delight. What a stroke of luck!

Hold it! What was that? A Red Alert from my mental command center. The purring had stopped! Instinctively, I cowered down in the litter on the bottom of my cage.

And then I heard it: a sound so faint that even my sharp ears had trouble detecting it. It was the sound of ultra-soft

paws approaching from the next room. I heard the door being pushed open a little, and the sound increased in volume. I could guess its source.

Worming my way to the front of the cage, I cautiously peered over the edge. Sure enough, the apparition below my bookshelf made me quake with terror.

IT WAS WILLIAM.

He was the biggest, blackest tomcat I'd ever seen. His huge green eyes were gazing up at me, and they seemed to convey a message: "If I want to get you, I will." After a while he turned and padded off — slowly, with his tail in the air.

I beat a wary retreat and crawled into my burrow. Stay cool, Freddy! — that, yet again, was the order of the day.

The bars of my cage would undoubtedly withstand the teeth of a tomcat, however strong, so I was safe inside. But on the outside? Never. In the age-old contest between cat and hamster, the cat always wins, quite simply because its teeth are bigger and its jaws more powerful.

I couldn't afford to venture outside the cage. In other

words, I would never be able to get at the treasure trove
of books all around me.

It was awful. I literally wrung my little paws in
despair. Melancholy overcame me once more, this time
to such an extent that I sank into a kind of hibernating
stupor.

I was roused by some strange noises. They were very

loud and quite close to me. What could they be? No matter how depressed I was feeling, I had to find out. I crawled out of my burrow.

It was Mr. John. He was taking some books from the shelf, right beside my cage, and putting them in his leather briefcase.

"Well, kid, settled in already?" He gave me a nod and left the room. Moments later I heard the front door open and shut. A key was turned twice in the lock, then footsteps descended the stairs. Mr. John was going someplace. Melancholy overwhelmed me once more as I turned to reenter my burrow —

aND THEN I HEARD THE SONG.

CHAPTER TEN

IT WASN'T A SONG AT FIRST, to be precise, just the whistling duet I'd heard before. But then Enrico and Caruso stopped whistling and started singing — quite loudly, at that. With remorseless persistence, they belted out their ditty from beginning to end:

"All day long we sing our song
and whistle as we do so.
No guinea pigs sing sweeter than
Enrico and Caruso.

A hamster doesn't sing, it squeaks
and stuffs its cheeks with fodder
until they swell up like balloons.
No creature could look odder.

But guinea pigs, they sing their song
and whistle as they do so.
Nicer by far than hamsters are
Enrico and Caruso."

I stiffened. "No creature could look odder. . . ." The nerve of them! How dare those impudent guinea pigs include me in their lousy song! How dare they poke fun at me in that hymn to self-glorification!

I bared my teeth and snarled with rage. They broadcast their opinions to the world while the likes of me had to listen to them — in fact I would have to listen to them whenever they felt like it. Again and again and again . . . I was at their mercy.

That was when I blew a fuse. Working at top speed, I unearthed my pencil and hauled the carousel into position. The cage door opened with a click, and I swiftly climbed down, paw over paw, to the floor. Then I scampered off to give Enrico and Caruso a piece of my mind.

All at once, however, William loomed up ahead of me.

To help my human readers picture how huge a gigantic tomcat looks to a hamster, I should here point out that, by human standards, William was the size of a house.

In such a situation, two possible courses of action present themselves. The first is to fall over backward, stick all four paws in the air, and pretend to be dead. My mental command center opted for the second alternative.

I rose on my hind legs, made myself as tall as possible, and blew out my cheeks. This is supposed to double a hamster's size and tell an enemy, "I'm not to be messed with."

William didn't pounce on me, as it happened. He stayed where he was — indeed, he actually sat down. This encouraged me to draw myself up some more.

"Listen to me, tomcat," I told him. Suddenly overcome with a kind of reckless abandon, I added, "If that's what you still are. A tomcat, I mean."

William's eyes narrowed. He stood up and loomed

over me once more. Then he spoke in a surprisingly reso-
nant but gentle voice.

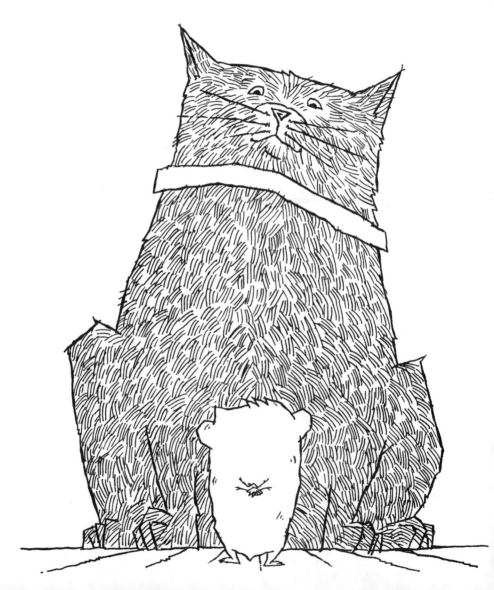

"If you mean I've been neutered," he said quietly, "let me tell you this: All truly civilized tomcats are neutered. That's point one. Point two," he went on, unsheathing his claws, each of which was longer than one of my legs, "— point two, to be frank, is that I find it quite absurd for a five-inch hamster to try to play the lion tamer with a cat my size. So kindly drop the act. Then, maybe, we can have a civilized conversation."

"Oof!" I said, expelling the air from my cheek pouches.

William cocked his head a little. "You're Freddy, I presume."

I nodded. "And you're William."

"Sir William."

"Huh?"

"SiR WiLLiaM, if you please."

Well, why not? No one who has just escaped death should object to a little word like *Sir*. Why hadn't I introduced myself as Freddy Auratus? Then he could have addressed me as *Mr.* Auratus.

"Everyone calls me *Sir* William," William said loftily.

I'm prejudiced against arrogant snobs as a rule, but it didn't do to be ungrateful. The dreaded cat-versus-hamster duel hadn't taken place, nor would it in the future. I was safe. I could leave my cage freely!

"Congratulations, by the way," said Sir William.

I was puzzled. "On what?"

"On getting your cage door open. In my experience, it's the first time one of you rodents has ever performed such a feat."

"Thanks." I felt genuinely flattered, I admit.

Just in case it's of interest to my readers, we were communicating in Interanimal, a kind of telepathic dialect. To the best of my knowledge, all mammals can speak it. Except for humans, of course.

"And now," said Sir William, "it's time you introduced yourself to the other inmates."

The other inmates? "Enrico and Caruso, you mean? But, Sir William, is that, er, absolutely essential?"

"Of course," he said, his green eyes surveying me

intently. "They're part of the family. You'll like them. I'm sure you heard them singing just now. Charming, wasn't it? They're amusing little fellows, always good-tempered and fond of cracking jokes. Rather smelly, though, in my opinion."

Well, at least he'd noticed it too. I congratulated myself on not having blurted out my own opinion of the pair. That might have blighted the atmosphere.

We went into the room next door. It was strange, but I hardly noticed Sir William's smell anymore, whereas the smell of guinea pigs' pee-pee stung my nostrils more and more the nearer we got. And there they were.

Mr. John had kindly presented the guinea pigs with a

large cage whose floor was strewn with lettuce leaves. Not a sign of systematic hoarding, and as for the damp patches all over the floor . . . enough said! One of the guinea pigs was big and plump and had short black-and-white fur. The other was smaller, with a long red-and-white coat concealing a rather scrawny body. They both sat up and looked at us. They said nothing, but their little black eyes darted to and fro.

"That," said Sir William, jerking his head at the little red-and-white one, "is Enrico. And that," he said, indicating the fat black-and-white one, "is Caruso." Their beady eyes continued to dart to and fro.

"Gentlemen," Sir William went on, "permit me to introduce the new addition to our family. This is Freddy."

"Full name: Freddy Auratus," I took the liberty of adding.

They exchanged a look, then burst out laughing. "Auratus," squealed scrawny Enrico. "Hip, hip, hurratus!"

"Freddy Hurratus, Freddy Hurratus!" fat Caruso chimed in. They clung to each other, squealing with laughter.

Sir William nodded at me and smiled. "Well," his expression conveyed, "was I exaggerating?"

No.

Not, at least, where their fondness for cracking jokes was concerned, though the quality of those jokes was, of course, a matter of opinion. I lifted one corner of my mouth and twitched the appropriate whiskers. This might have signified all manner of things, but Enrico and Caruso took it the way it was intended.

"Oho," said Enrico, "I get it: Mr. Freddy Auratus doesn't share our sense of humor. He's hard to please."

Caruso faked sorrow. "Looks like we'll have to be a whole lot funnier," he said, "or he'll boo us off the stage."

Enrico clasped one paw to his brow in a tragic pose. "Alas, what

have we done to deserve such an unappreciative audience?"

And they hugged one another once more, beside themselves with mirth.

"Well," Sir William told them, smiling, "I feel sure you're going to get along splendidly with our new inmate. And now, Freddy, I'll show you around the apartment. See you later, gentlemen."

"Farewell, Fearless Fred!" Enrico cried dramatically.

"Remind me to give you a kiss the next time!" chortled Caruso.

Squeals of laughter followed us out of the room.

Sir William was still smiling. Either he had a rather underdeveloped sense of humor, or his feline refinement prompted him to take a tolerant view of their wisecracks. In any event, it was clear that the guinea pigs were under his protection. This made it easier for me simply to ignore the pair instead of falling out with them.

"Mr. John found those two —"

"You also call him Mr. John?" I asked.

"Yes, ever since we got to know little Sophie. Anyway, Mr. John spotted them in the window of a seedy pet shop. They were thoroughly neglected. He felt so sorry for them, he bought them, and we gave them a home here." Guessing what I would ask next, Sir William added, "I've been with Mr. John for ages — years, in fact." He paused and looked around. "This is the living room. This is where I live and sleep. Nice, isn't it?"

I gave a vague nod. With eyes like mine I couldn't see as far as the nearest table leg, of course, but I resolved to explore the whole place later at my leisure.

"Enrico and Caruso live here too, unfortunately." Sir William looked at me. "Don't get me wrong, please. I'm very fond of them, but there's the smell problem. It doesn't seem to bother Mr. John." He sighed. "Ah well, one gets used to it in the end. This way, please."

We went back into the room where my cage was. "This," Sir William explained, "is the study. It's where Mr. John works on his translations. Mostly from German to English."

105

"I see," I said.

Sir William swiveled his broad tomcat's head in my direction. "Forgive me, my dear Freddy, but I doubt if you've got the faintest idea what I'm talking about."

"Well," I said, "maybe I have, a little. Mr. John converts German reading matter into English. Since he speaks English all the time, I guess he must find that easier than the other way around."

"Well I never!" Sir William had come to a halt. "Am I wrong, or are you speaking as an expert on the written word?"

I tried to explain as modestly but as clearly as possible. "It's true, Sir William, I can't deny it. I *have* learned to read a little. In fact," I added, "I can read whole books."

"You don't say!" Sir William shook his head. "A little rodent like you, reading whole books? I'm at a loss for words." He looked down at me from his great height. "No, honestly, I take my hat off to you. There are times when I wish I could read myself. On the other hand, it wouldn't really suit me somehow, would it?"

Pardon me, I felt like saying, *but what do you mean? Anyone who doesn't learn to read is either too dumb or too lazy.*

"Anyway," Sir William went on, "there's no need for me to learn, now that we've got an expert on the premises."

"Hmm," was all I said. If he expected me to read him bedtime stories, he was making a big mistake.

"So," said Sir William, "we still haven't toured the kitchen, bathroom, and hallway, but I'm afraid we'll have to postpone that. Mr. John will be back soon, and he mustn't catch you outside your cage."

"Of course not — I mean, *why* not? Why shouldn't I have the run of the apartment? *You* do, after all."

"In cases like this, my dear Freddy, my late father used to say, '*Quod licet Jovi non licet bovi.*' That's Latin, and it means roughly, 'Almighty God is allowed to do things forbidden to ordinary mortals.' You'd never catch *me* saying such a thing, of course." Sir William gave a suave smile. "Seriously, though," he went on, "if anyone lets you out it must be Mr. John. Being a human, he'd object if you got out by yourself." He pricked his ears. "Aside from that," he said, speaking rather quickly now, "I'd advise you not to let him see how you open your cage door. You never know how things will turn out. And now, back into your cage. Quick, he's coming up the stairs."

I could hear him too, now. Sir William's ears seemed to be even sharper than mine. Off I went. I darted over to the bookshelves — and stopped short. My cage was on the third shelf up, and that was miles above me. I'd climbed down with ease, because I was so furious, but how to climb up?

"I was afraid of this." Sir William had stationed himself beside me. "I'm really too old for this sort of thing, but still . . ." He lowered his head. "All right, on you get. And grip my fur tightly in your teeth."

I did so, and while I was savoring the very peculiar taste that began to pervade my mouth, Sir William performed a gigantic leap that landed us on the shelf beside my cage. "We'll have to think of some other method," he panted, "but not now. Into your cage, quick!" I had only

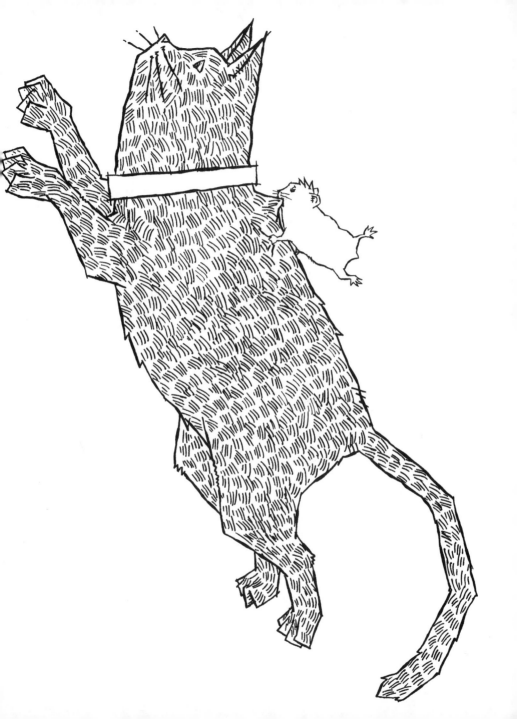

just clambered into the cage when he lifted the door with his paw and snapped the catch into place. He obviously knew the way it was done, but how?

He jumped down. "Don't forget to bury that pencil," he called from the floor. He must have been watching me from the outset. If so, he probably realized I'd left my cage because I was so furious with Enrico and Caruso, but had politely overlooked the fact. I could count myself very fortunate to have come across a civilized tomcat in Mr. John's home, instead of a bloodthirsty predator. I looked down at him once more, and he gave me a friendly wink.

I had just buried the pencil when Mr. John came in.

"No, William," he said, shaking his head, "Freddy's not for you. Be a good boy and stick to canned food."

CHAPTER ELEVEN

"FEELING HOLLOW, KID?" asked Mr. John. I wasn't sure I'd understood him correctly. To be on the safe side, I scampered over to my feeding place and sat up and begged. Mr. John nodded and went out. Sure enough, a few moments later he came back with some food. It was precisely my usual mixture. That was welcome in one way but less welcome in another. Why? Because there still weren't any mealworms. It would have been great simply to be able to let Mr. John know this.

I could have also let him know that I was interested in his books but had absolutely no intention of nibbling them, and that he might be able to help me get the books I wanted off the shelf (because I could foresee a few problems arising in that respect), and that . . . Oh, there were so many things I could have told him. Suddenly, what struck me as my main priority was this: I had to get in touch with Mr. John.

Except that I didn't have the faintest idea how to do so.

Mr. John had gone next door again. Enrico and Caruso were obviously being fed, because I could hear them whistling shrilly. Then Sir William started purring, which presumably meant that he was being fed as well.

Mr. John came back into the study. I saw as he passed the bookshelves that he was carrying a tray with a coffeepot and a cup on it and several apples lying beside them. He put the tray on the big desk that stood against the wall beside the window. I had seen this during my tour of inspection with Sir William, but only as a towering structure from below. I now noticed that it was piled high with books.

Mr. John sat down at the desk. I naturally expected him to pick up a pencil and start writing. Not single words or short sentences, like Sophie — no, he would surely translate whole books into English.

But Mr. John didn't reach for a pencil. Turning to a smaller, lower table beside him, he picked up something that seemed quite heavy and deposited it on his desk — a

machine, from the look of it. I could make out a sort of
roller, black at the edges and white in the middle, but
most of the contraption appeared to consist of a lot of
round keys arranged in rows, like steps.

Mr. John opened a book and put it down beside the machine. Then he sat looking at it for a while, quite motionless. Suddenly he raised his hands, stuck out both forefingers, and brought them down on the machine. His fingers landed on the keys, some levers shot up, and a series of loud, unpleasant clattering sounds rang out. He repeated this procedure a number of times, then stared at the open book again. What on earth was he doing?

I mean, I guessed he was translating, but I confess I observed his behavior for a long time with total incomprehension. The truth didn't dawn on me until he reached into the machine, pulled out a sheet of paper, and held it up in front of his eyes as if reading. Of course, he *was* reading! And then I got it: Mr. John had been writing! He didn't use a pencil to write with, like Sophie, but a machine. In order to write with it, you simply had to press the keys down. Humans did this with their fingers, but any kind of weight would do. The weight of a golden hamster, for instance.

I COULD WRITE TOO!

It was like a gate being flung open before my eyes. Looking through it, I seemed to see a road that would take me on a fantastic journey to a bright and glorious country in the distance — the Promised Land, I thought suddenly. There in the distance lay the Promised Land of Assyria. I couldn't tell exactly what it looked like, not yet, but one thing was certain: It would bear no resemblance to Great-Grandmother's imaginings.

Well, so much for my daydreams. Present reality was less bright and glorious — in fact it became more somber still. The longer I watched Mr. John at his typewriter and saw how he not only pressed the keys down but positively punched them with his fingers, the more I realized that I could never manage to write that way with my weight alone. To make the levers clatter, I would have had to land on the keys from a height of at least three feet — not to mention the difficulty of hitting the right ones.

I needed help, and that I could only get from Sir William.

I had to wait until nightfall. Mr. John spent all day working on his translation. Once or twice Sir William sauntered in, jumped up on the desk and settled down among the books, purring loudly, only to disappear once more into the room next door. He avoided looking in my direction and behaved as if I didn't interest him in the least, presumably because he didn't want to alarm Mr. John.

When evening came, Mr. John gathered up his books, stowed them in his briefcase, and left the apartment. I later discovered that he not only translated books but also gave private lessons in German.

I pried open my cage door in no time. Getting down to ground level took considerably longer. Even when not in a rage, however, I managed to mountaineer, paw over paw, from shelf to shelf. I thanked my lucky stars I'd always kept myself in shape with my gym equipment, but the study was dark by the time I finally made it to the floor.

Having memorized the route to the door, I reached the next room comparatively quickly. For some reason, I had thought that finding Sir William there would present no problem.

NO SUCH LUCK.

I ran this way and that, pausing now and then to listen. Whenever he wasn't purring, however, Sir William evidently made no sound at all. I had his scent in my nostrils, of course, but that was too universal to enable me to locate him. Enrico and Caruso were only too easy to locate, on the other hand, but I'd be darned if I would go any nearer those jokers than I absolutely had to. That was why I didn't call Sir William's name. I knew only too well what the result would be.

In the end, though, I had no choice.

"Sir William?" At first I spoke softly, hoping he was somewhere near me. No answer. "Sir William?" Louder, but still no answer. "Sir William!"

That did it.

"Hark, hark!" Enrico cried. "I heard a voice a-calling in the dark."

"Ah yes," Caruso chimed in, "methinks it was a hamster in distress."

"He wants Sir William, or my ears deceive me."

"And we alone can help you, Fred, believe me."

"But only if you deign to be polite."

"If not, good riddance and good night."

They relapsed into silence. No laughter, nothing. So they could be quiet as mice if they chose. I was loath to admit it, but I was impressed by that ad-lib performance of theirs. It seemed that even their undisciplined minds could bear fruit occasionally. All the same, I was careful not to make a sound. I refused to fall into their trap. They wanted to involve me in something that wasn't my cup of tea. Hamsters didn't hunker down in pee-pee-sodden litter and laze their lives away.

On the other hand, I was anxious to find Sir William. Where could he be? Not all that far away, surely. Should I call him again? No, those guinea pigs would laugh themselves silly. But there was no alternative. I had to take the bull by the horns — I had to confront the guinea pigs in their den.

My eyes were now so used to the darkness, I could see their cage. I drew a deep breath and darted over to it. Once there I drew myself up, blew out my cheeks, emitted a snarl — and they fell over backward. They simply fell flat on their backs, overcome with fright, and lay there.

Yes, guinea pigs may be impudent individuals, but they've got no guts. The sight of a combat-ready hamster had reduced those two to silence — or almost, I should add, because the power of speech didn't desert them even then.

Still lying there, Enrico had the nerve to cry, "Mercy, mercy, Your Hamstership!"

Caruso guffawed. "If I were you, Your Hamstership, I wouldn't eat me. I'm dietarily inadvisable: too much cholesterol." And the pair of them clutched their tummies, shrieking with laughter.

119

"Okay," I snapped. "You've had your fun. Now I want an answer. Where do I find Sir William?"

"No, no." With a grunt, Caruso grabbed one of the bars of the cage and hauled himself to his feet. "We can't let His Hamstership go without giving him a present. Know what I mean, partner?"

"A song!" cried Enrico. "We'll send him on his way with a song!"

I tried to keep my cool. "Listen, you guys. That's enough, okay? Tell me where Sir William is and I'll leave you in peace."

"Leave us in peace, will you? Great. But we won't leave *you* in peace, Your Hamstership." Caruso managed to look almost angry, and Enrico squeaked, "You listen to our song, we give you the info, is it a deal?"

What choice did I have? I nodded, and they launched into "All day long we sing our song."

I was made to listen to every last verse. It became apparent, as I watched them singing, that they weren't being deliberately malicious; they simply thought their song the finest ever composed and were eager to sing it. It never crossed their minds that someone like me might find it offensive. But that would not have made a difference, far from it. Guinea pigs are not only impudent, uncouth, and gutless; they're conceited as well.

The song came to an end at last. I was curious to know what else they'd cooked up for me. "Well," I said with a self-control that surprised me, "may I now be permitted to know Sir William's whereabouts?"

Enrico nodded. "Sure."

"So where is he?"

"Right behind you," said Caruso.

I spun around. And there sat Sir William, his green eyes glowing in the darkness.

CHapTeR TWeLVe

"AS I EXPECT YOU KNOW," said Sir William, "we cats can see in the dark." He paused, widening his eyes so they glowed even brighter. "I've been watching you for quite a while."

Quite a while? Had I, without knowing it, been subjected to some kind of test? I glanced around at Enrico and Caruso, but they seemed to be waiting in silence for whatever would happen next.

With a jerk of the head, Sir William signaled to me to follow and led the way into the study, which was lighter than the living room. As I followed that enormous black tomcat through the gloom, I couldn't help feeling rather uneasy despite myself.

Once in the study, Sir William came to a halt. "I'll be brief," he said. "You really scared Enrico and Caruso just now. Hamsters are capable of looking warlike, but guinea pigs are defenseless creatures. Do you know what your type of behavior is called?" He looked at me as if expecting an answer, so I shook my head. "Bullying," he said, "that's what it's called." He spread his paws so the claws protruded. "Just so we understand each other, there's a rule in Mr. John's home, and that rule is: No bullying."

Great. So what did he call those jokers' song?

"Do I make myself clear?" asked Sir William.

I nodded. He evidently thought it was quite all right for the guinea pigs to provoke me, so I held my tongue. After all, I wanted something out of the big cat.

"Good," said Sir William, "that's settled, then. And now, my friend, tell me why you wanted a word with me."

Heaven alone knew. Had there been the slightest chance of coping with the problem on my own, I would have simply left him standing there. As it was, I said, "I have a problem, Sir William. I'd very much like to write with Mr. John's typewriter, but I'm not strong enough to use it."

"You want to write?" Sir William eyed me keenly. Then he smiled. "Behold our expert on the written word — he only feels happy when he's messing around with letters and so on. Very praise worthy of you. If you'll pardon my saying so, however, it betrays a rather one-track mind."

I was positively fascinated by Sir William's display of superiority, but I kept my temper. "I hardly think," I said, "that it betrays a one-track mind to want to get in touch with Mr. John."

"Oh." He regarded me thoughtfully. "Is that really what you're after? Hmm." He glanced at the desk with the typewriter on it. "Very well. Then we'd better take a look, hadn't we?" He lowered his head. "On you get."

I climbed onto his head, hung on tight with my teeth, and we landed beside the machine. Getting down on the desktop, I rose on my hind legs. It was just as I had fore-seen: Each of the round keys bore a single letter. I placed one forepaw on the X and the other on the Y. "You have to press them down one at a time, see?" I said. "That way, you can string whole words together."

"I'm not entirely unaware of that, my friend. I too

have been privileged to watch Mr. John at work from time to time." Sir William smiled one of his suave smiles. "And now, I imagine, you're hoping I'll press the keys down for you. Am I right?"

I nodded, quite startled. It was all going swimmingly — far better than I'd expected. "It would be tremendously kind of you."

He gave me a thoughtful look. "There are only two snags. In the first place, I'm not an expert on the written word, as you know."

126

"No problem there. I'll show you which keys to press."

"Hmm . . . Even if I went along with that, there's still the second snag. Look." Sir William placed his right forepaw on the keyboard. It covered not only the H in the center but the G on the left, the J on the right, and the B and N below.

I stared at his huge paw, feeling rather foolish. Quite clearly, the typewriter wasn't designed for it. I should have thought of that, of course. Then I had an idea.

"Your claws!" I exclaimed. "You could punch the keys with one of your claws."

Sir William shook his head. "I can't put them out one at a time, I'm afraid. And besides, I would never run the risk, to be frank. If my claws snapped off I would lose my identity."

"You'd lose your *what*?"

"My identity. I wouldn't be myself anymore. Even a civilized tom is still a tom, but a clawless tom is just a pussycat."

He was right, I guess, but that wasn't my problem. So what now? How could I press those keys down?

"Well, fancy that: Freddy the expert has run out of ideas." Sir William smirked. "I'm surprised you haven't hit on the obvious solution."

"Which is?" I asked, genuinely excited now.

"We simply lengthen the keys — with a cork, for instance. I'm sure there'll be one in the trash can. You stand the cork on the relevant key and hold it in position while —"

"— while you press it down!" I broke in.

"BINGO!"

That was it — he'd solved my writing problem in an instant.

"YIPPIDY-DOO!"

I cried. I leaped into the air and turned a somersault before landing. "I can write!"

"So it seems." Sir William's smile suddenly vanished. "That's to say," he added gravely, "you *could* write" — he paused — "*if* I cooperated."

"W — what do you mean?"

"I mean I won't." He looked at me. "I won't help you write."

"But . . ." My plans collapsed like a house of cards. "Why on earth not?"

Sir William said nothing for a while, just stared at the keyboard. Then he turned away. "Because it wouldn't be right," he said.

"What wouldn't be right?" I demanded rather sharply. The mighty tomcat had evidently decided that it was beneath his dignity to assist a smart but very diminutive rodent. It was time to redetermine the relationship between physical strength and intellectual ability.

"It wouldn't be right to establish contact with a human."

"What?" The old gentleman had started talking nonsense, it seemed. "You must be joking," I said angrily. *"You* make it clear to Mr. John when you're hungry. If that isn't establishing contact, what is?"

"I don't like your tone, my little friend." Sir William fixed me with his glowing green eyes. "You're right, I *do* establish contact with him, but I do so in my own way: I purr or meow. What you have in mind is a form of contact established by human means, and that isn't right."

"Why should one be right and the other not?" I asked, controlling myself with an effort.

"Because it's beneath an animal's dignity. It's undignified even to imitate a human. Take those animals in zoos that beg for food by waving their paws around: contemptible! As for trying to communicate with humans in their own language, that's positively reprehensible. What are the most pathetic creatures in the world?"

"Talking parrots," I reluctantly conceded. "But, Sir William, if only I could use that typewriter —"

"That's enough! I refuse to discuss it further." Sir

William frowned, then suddenly yawned. "Hi-ho," he said, "I must be off to my blanket and you to your burrow. All right, on you get."

I was back in my cage before I knew it. "Good night," said Sir William, shutting the door with a click. He jumped off the bookshelf and disappeared.

I sat there, utterly defeated. There were no two ways around it. I couldn't do any writing.

Melancholy overcame me once more, but this time I fought back. Get lost, I told it. And, when Melancholy asked what right I had to send it packing, I said: In the first place, I know how writing works in principle. That's a great deal in itself. Second, I know Sir William is wrong. Even a wise tomcat's powers of imagination are limited, and Sir William is extremely narrow-minded — at least where the subject of "contact with humans" is concerned. Third, I've decided not to let every last little setback cast me down into a bottomless pit of despair. Stay cool, Freddy! — that's still the order of the day.

Next, I gave myself a pep talk. Okay, Freddy, I said,

you may not be able to write, but you can still read. There are books all around you: right, left, above, below — enough books to last a hamster's lifetime. You're in a book-lover's paradise, so get reading!

It worked.

I shelved the subject of writing, so to speak, and turned to that of reading. And then, as if anything more were needed to keep me on my toes, I was promptly confronted by the need to solve a rather fundamental problem.

The books were standing upright in rows, side by side. How could I maneuver the book I wanted to read into a position where I could turn the pages? More to the point, how could I do so without alerting Mr. John? Sir William had been absolutely right about one thing: Mr. John mustn't discover my pencil. After all, who could tell when I might need it in an emergency?

I toiled away all evening, but in vain. I was simply too small and too weak to pull a book out, let alone lay it down flat. I didn't give up, though. The next evening I set

to work again. Suddenly, Sir William appeared on the shelf beside me.

"I don't object to you reading," he said, "so tell me which book you're after." I pointed to one at random. Sir William laid the book on its side and opened it. "If I hear Mr. John coming," he said, "I'll jump up and put it back." I nodded, and he jumped down again.

133

The book was called *The Forsyte Saga*. It was bound to contain plenty of reading matter, being one of the thickest, and it appeared to be about a human family whose members were always getting on one another's nerves. Very appropriate, I thought, recalling my time with Sophie, Gregory, and Mom. "Part One," I read. "Chapter One: 'At home' at Old Jolyon's . . ."

That was the start of a wonderfully stimulating journey through my book-lover's paradise.

Every evening, when Mr. John had left the apartment (as he did most evenings), the same thing happened: Sir William jumped onto the bookshelf, pried open my cage door with his claws (which saved me from having to mess around with the pencil), opened whichever book I pointed to, and disappeared. The next two or three hours were my own. I sat at the foot of the book and devoured page after page in the dim but adequate light that filtered through the study window.

It was terribly slow going at first, I have to admit, especially as *The Forsyte Saga* was very tough fare for a beginner. However, once I had learned to read on instead of getting bogged down in passages that resisted my powers of comprehension, I became quite as skilled at reading as Mr. John himself. I tackled one book after another. My evening sessions regularly ended the way Sir William had predicted. As soon as he heard Mr. John on the stairs Sir William jumped up beside me, replaced the book, and closed my cage door.

Sometimes he turned up early. "Well, my friend," he would say, "still hard at it? Take care you don't ruin your eyesight." Sir William was fond of shooting the breeze.

When I told him what I happened to be reading he would listen awhile, then shake his head and say, "Amazing how much a little rodent's head can hold." He not only looked upon my reading as the pastime of an eccentric expert but tolerated it as patiently as he tolerated Enrico's and Caruso's wisecracks.

I saw no reason to climb down from my bookshelf, so I never set eyes on the guinea pigs during this period. I heard them, though, because they performed their song from time to time. Although I still involuntarily bared my teeth whenever I heard it, I was becoming hardened to their jokes at my expense.

But then they started playing games.

It happened after Sophie had paid me a visit.

CHAPTER THIRTEEN

I'D BEEN LIVING AT MR. JOHN's for five days when Sophie reappeared for the first time, probably because Mom had kept her too busy to come sooner. She turned up one afternoon. Mr. John was sitting at his desk, reading, and Sir William had settled down among his master's books. I was jogging on the carousel when I suddenly heard her footsteps on the stairs. I raced to the door of my cage and sat up to show how much I'd been looking forward to seeing her. I fidgeted with excitement. Then it occurred to me that my fur might be tousled, so I started cleaning myself vigorously.

Sir William looked over at me with a grin.

There was a knock on the front door, and Mr. John went out. "Hi, kid," I heard him say. "Nice to see you."

"Hello, Mr. John." That was Sophie's voice. "How's Freddy?"

"Oh, he's fine, I guess. Come in and see for yourself."

There she was at last. The familiar scent of sunflower seeds filled my nostrils. It was my Sophie, all right.

"Freddy!" She came running over to the cage. "Hello, Freddy."

I raised one paw as high as I could, and then — casting dignity to the winds —

I WAVED TO HER.

She beamed. "He's saying hello! Look, Mr. John, he's waving to me!"

"I've never seen him do that before," said Mr. John. "He must like you a lot."

That, Mr. John, was putting it mildly.

"Here, Freddy, I've brought you something." Sophie held up a paper bag. "Something really special." She opened the door of the cage. "My book on golden hamsters says it's a delicacy."

A delicacy? Could it possibly be a . . .

She emptied the contents of the paper bag onto my feeding place.

It really was a mealworm.

Sitting beside my feeding place after Sophie had gone, I still couldn't take it in. To think she'd done such a thing!

WHaT JOY!

I don't mean the mealworm itself, although naturally that

had been scrumptious. No, I mean the thought that lay behind it. The fact that she had figured out what would give me a treat — a really special one. To think she'd even looked it up in her book on golden hamsters, and all for my sake! I heaved a blissful sigh.

"Aaah . . ."

"Oooh . . ."

Two more sighs, this time from the room next door. I rose on my hind legs and stiffened.

"Ah, me," sighed Enrico. "A sound more wistful never reached my ears."

"Yes indeed," sighed Caruso. "Young Fred's a slave to passion, it appears."

"He's genuinely in love, from what I heard."

"A hamster and a little girl? Absurd!"

"An ill-matched pair, Enrico, I agree."

"His love is doomed to failure, can't he see?"

"Unless he's very careful, more's the pity —"

"— he'll wind up like the hamster in our ditty."

Whereupon they broke into song again:

"His lovesick heart throbs in his breast,
his little knees go weak.
He waves his tiny paw at her.
Ah, would that he could speak!
She smiles at him and says hello,
but he can only squeak."

There followed the inevitable squeals of laughter, and this time they sounded positively evil.

So what? I sat there cleaning my fur, quite relaxed, until a sudden fit of anger made me bare my teeth and snarl.

HOW DARE THEY!

How dare those uncouth louts drag my finer feelings through the mire! If I snatched up the pencil and pried open my

door, got into their cage, and gave them a thorough nip-
ping, I doubted if they would ever get fresh with me
again. Lucky for them Sir William was around. Okay, I
told myself, cool it.

But, angry though I was, I had to hand it to them. They
were on the ball, those two. That last poem had sounded
really good — quite professional. Enrico and Caruso
couldn't read, either of them, so they must have made it
up themselves. If guinea pigs could do that, making up
rhymes couldn't be all that hard.

What if I tried it myself? What if I fired some insulting
poems back at them? That would make those jokers sit up.
They would return my fire, of course, and the result
would be an instant war of words. But that was just what
they wanted. No thanks, the pair of you, count me out.

So what had I been thinking of, before they spoiled my
train of thought? Of course, I could recall it now: that
yummy mealworm Sophie brought. Thought, brought . . .
Good heavens, a rhyme! But no, this was ridiculous. If I
was going to make up a poem, I would do it properly. My

poem must be a genuine poem. Not just a joke, but one that put my emotions into words. I retired to my burrow and got down to it.

After an hour, almost to the minute, I had — well, no, not made up a poem, but come to the conclusion that a golden hamster was quite incapable of doing what seemed to come naturally to a pair of uncouth guinea pigs. Every rhyme I made up sounded as if I had tried to turn the instructions on a packet of hamster food into verse. Okay, so I couldn't make up poetry. But I could read. Why not see how the pros did it?

That evening, after Sir William had opened the door of my cage, I asked him to wait while I checked the backs of the books on my shelf. A surprising number of titles included the word *Poems*. I eventually opted for a small, slender volume whose pages I would be able to skim through quickly, and Sir William pulled it out for me.

When he had gone I opened the book and looked for a short poem that would vividly describe my feelings. I turned the pages. It seemed to be a collection of poems by different people, but some of them were terribly long-winded. One, which went on for verse after verse, began: "In Xanadu did Kubla Khan a stately pleasure-dome decree . . ." I read it through from beginning to end. All very colorful and interesting, but not up my alley and far too long. I continued to turn the pages.

Hey, how about this one? Only four lines, but they hit the nail on the head. Bingo! I had my poem:

A mighty pain to love it is,
and 'tis a pain that pain to miss;
but of all pains the greatest pain
it is to love, but love in vain.

I sat there, staring at the page and brooding. What of the future? What were my chances of expressing how I felt? Very poor. The most I could do, when Sophie came to visit, was to give her a little wave, and that was less than satisfactory. If only I could give her that poem to read. . . . Okay, so she might not get my meaning at all. Then again, she might. In any event, I ought to give it a try.

But it was no use. I couldn't write, so I couldn't make myself understood.

Stone walls do not a prison make,
nor iron bars a cage . . .

So ran another, more hopeful-sounding poem in the book. Maybe the poet was right, but it wasn't much of a comfort. I decided to give up reading for the night. Sir William could replace the book and shut my cage door himself. I crawled into my burrow and curled up in its depths.

How could I get to write?

SOMETHING HAD TO HAPPEN, BUT WHAT?

CHAPTER FOURTEEN

IT HAPPENED WHEN I HAD BEEN at Mr. John's for exactly two weeks. And it all began with a thud.

I was still asleep at noon when this sudden commotion woke me up and the whole burrow shook. I darted out into the open. Mr. John was right beside the bookshelves, and standing on the shelf next to my cage was — the typewriter.

Could he possibly have guessed that I wanted to learn to write? Had he devised some ingenious method of solving the problem? I rose on my hind legs and clung to the cage door.

"Sorry I woke you, kid," he said, "but I had to get this old thing off my desk. I need the space."

Hmm, maybe I'd been wrong about his intentions. But what did he need the space for? What did he have in mind?

Mr. John left the room. He opened the front door but didn't shut it. Then I heard him hurry down the stairs.

After a while he returned, but his footsteps were labored and he was breathing heavily. He reached the top of the stairs at last, kicked the door open, and came tottering in with an enormous cardboard box. Groaning under its weight, he put it down on the floor and disappeared again.

Printed on the box were lots of words and symbols that meant nothing to me. What on earth did *monitor* signify? Mr. John came panting back up the stairs with a slightly less enormous cardboard box, which he deposited on the small table. Last of all, he fetched three cardboard boxes, one on top of the other, and put them on the desk: a medium-size one, a flat one, and a small one. Then he sat down, drew a deep breath, and surveyed them all. I couldn't wait for him to unpack them.

He began with the biggest box. Out came, first, a lot of packaging, and then the thing called a monitor, which resembled a television set. He heaved it onto the desk. From the slightly smaller package he extracted a gray metal box, which he put under the table. Then he turned his attention to the three remaining cardboard boxes.

149

Laying the small and medium-size ones aside, he opened the flat one. This contained what looked like — yes, a typewriter!

"Hello?" The telephone had rung. Mr. John held the new typewriter in his hand as he spoke, so I was able to get a good view of it. "Yes," he said, "I'm just unpacking it."

The new typewriter was gray instead of black and very much flatter than the old one. I couldn't figure out where you rolled the paper in.

"Of course, but you can come over anyway."

The new typewriter consisted mainly of keys, like the old one, but they were square instead of round, and you could read the letters on them more easily.

"Oh, I see. . . . But he's settled in nicely here, I think. Another change of scene might be too stressful."

Square keys or round — what difference did it make? Writing with a machine required more strength than I possessed.

"Well, I can understand how Sophie feels. . . . Of course. See you in a minute." He hung up.

SOPHIE? WAS SHE GOING TO PAY ME A VISIT?

Mr. John proceeded to mess around with various cables. It seemed he was connecting the typewriter and the monitor to the metal box and the metal box to an outlet. Then he sat down and started to read a book he'd also unpacked. After a while he got up, opened the small cardboard box, and took out an object that looked like one of Sir William's paws, except that it was gray and bigger. He plugged this into the typewriter and put it down alongside it. Then he went on reading. For ages.

He certainly knew how to keep a curious hamster on pins and needles.

All at once he jumped up, hesitated for an instant, then reached for the typewriter and pressed a button. A gong sounded, there was a humming noise, and the monitor started to glow. Some mysterious symbols and pictures appeared on the screen. After a while Mr. John reached for the thing that resembled Sir William's paw, and I heard

it give a faint click. The screen underwent
another change, becoming as white as paper.

Mr. John sat down in front of the new
typewriter. He raised his hands and extended
both forefingers. But instead of punching the
keyboard with them, he dropped his wrists
and pressed the keys down quite gently.
Black letters appeared on the white screen
as if they were being printed on paper:
Mr. John was using his new machine to
write with.

As I watched him typing at

his desk and depressing the keys with very little effort, I realized that this was the machine for me. With *this* one, I *could* write!

Not long afterward I heard Sophie's footsteps on the stairs. Her visit didn't suit me at all, to be honest. I would much rather have continued to enjoy the sight of Mr. John typing so light-handedly. Besides, I had to figure out how to persuade Sir William that writing wasn't beneath a hamster's dignity, nor was using it to get in touch with Mr. John.

Sophie didn't appear to be alone. Her footsteps were accompanied by other, heavier footsteps.

There was a knock on the front door, and Mr. John went out. "Hi, kid," he said. Then, "Hello, Gregory."

Gregory? Of course, he was due back from his concert tour yesterday. But what was he doing here?

"Freddy!" Sophie came bursting into the study. "Just imagine, Freddy, you can come home!"

I'd have liked to say good-bye to Sir William, and also —
by some means or other — to Mr. John. Maybe even to
Enrico and Caruso as well. But Gregory and Sophie were
out of Mr. John's apartment with my cage before I
could so much as squeak.

Nothing in Sophie's bedroom had changed.
The schoolbooks and pencils on her desk
might never have been moved. Gregory
placed my cage on the shelf, exactly in
the same old place. As for Sophie, she
welcomed me back with three fat
mealworms.

She was the nicest girl in the
world, but her room was the
dullest place on earth.

I had been whisked off
into an intellectual
void — wrested
away from Mr. John's
new typewriter.

How I would cope with this disaster, I still didn't know. I hadn't managed to give it any thought, just gorged myself on the mealworms. But gorging instead of thinking wouldn't get me anything but a fat tummy. If I carried on that way I would simply swell up and burst.

I would have to adapt to the new situation as soon as possible.

It could have been worse. The shelves in Mom's bedroom were filled with books from floor to ceiling. How to lay them down flat and open them, now that I was solely dependent on my own efforts, was something I would discover in due time.

"Are you happy to be home again, Freddy?"

I sat up and begged, looking friendly.

She didn't have a clue, the dear girl, but she meant well.

"Sophie? Come here a minute, would you?"

"Yes, Mom." Sophie went out, leaving the door ajar.

"What did we agree on this morning, Sophie? Before I allowed you to bring your hamster home, I mean?"

I couldn't wait to hear.

"I must never let Freddy out of his cage."

Forget it, Mom. You're up against the Houdini of the hamster world.

"Correct. What else?"

"The door to my bedroom must always be kept shut."

"Exactly. So please remember that from now on."

"Yes, Mom." Sophie came back into the room, closing the door behind her.

The door was shut and would remain so. I would be a prisoner in Sophie's bedroom. All night and every night as well, and that meant —

"Oh, one more thing, Sophie," Mom called. Sophie opened the door again.

"Yes, Mom?"

"That cage — it smells. It needs a thorough spring-cleaning. You'd better change all the bedding."

Change the bedding? Then Sophie would find my pencil. Would she remember she'd given it to me as a present? Perhaps, but I couldn't count on that. If she took it away I wouldn't just be imprisoned in her bedroom. I'd be shut up in my cage forever.

"But, Mom, you threw away the bag of litter."

"Then your father will have to buy some more. In the meantime, ask John to let you have some. He's bound to keep a supply of litter for those guinea pigs of his."

"Yes, Mom, I'll go right away."

"No, call him. He won't mind bringing some over."

"But I'd rather go myself. Can I?" Mom reluctantly agreed, so Sophie left the room with a cheerful "See you later, Freddy."

That was my chance. There was only one thing left to do: **BREAK OUT.** I had to escape in double-quick time, before something else happened to prevent me.

I hesitated even so. Sophie would be sad. Freddy, her beloved golden hamster, would be gone. From the looks of it, he would simply have deserted her. Why? Hadn't he been well off where he was? Hadn't she always looked after him conscientiously? Sophie would be not only sad but really miserable.

What about me? I *wouldn't* be miserable to say good-bye to Sophie, but I *would* be miserable — thoroughly so — to be shut up in my cage for evermore.

I got out and climbed down the curtain in less than a minute. I didn't bother to close the cage door behind me. The pencil lay exposed on top of my bedding — it had served its purpose. But where should I hide? Where would Sophie look for me? I thought it over. Then I turned around and made my way back up the curtain. Instead of stopping on a level with the shelf, I continued to climb until I reached the valance. It was wide enough to provide me with a safe perch. No one would be able to see me from below.

As soon as I got a chance I would sneak out of Sophie's room and into the rest of the apartment. My next requirement would be a hideaway — one with sufficient room for a larder because, never knowing where my next meal would come from, I would have to hoard anything edible I came across. Foraging for food would take a lot of courage on my part. I would have to be constantly on my guard against discovery. I would have to roam all over the apartment too, so Mom would be bound to have another attack of her hamster-hair allergy. And that, I knew full well, would result in a merciless hunt for me.

I sidled to the edge of the valance. My cage was down there. The door stood invitingly open, and inside was the comfortable burrow in which I could still, if I chose, laze away the rest of my life in a well-fed stupor. I sidled back again.

Life on the run would be hard.

BUT I HaD NO CHOICE.

Not under present circumstances.

CHAPTER FIFTEEN

SOPHIE CAME BACK ACCOMPANIED by Mr. John. I watched them as I peeped warily over the edge of the valance. He had obviously been reluctant to let Sophie carry the bag of litter by herself, for what he had brought along could hardly be called a bag; it was more like a huge sack. He was carrying it clamped under one arm and his leather briefcase under the other.

"Well," he said, pushing the bedroom door shut with his foot. "Where shall we put the litter?"

But Sophie didn't reply. She was staring wide-eyed at my cage. "L-look," she stammered, "the door." Then she cried, "**FREDDY'S GONE!**"

"Oh." Mr. John put the bag of litter on Sophie's chair. "Easy, kid," he said. "Maybe he's in his burrow."

Sophie reached the cage in two strides. "Come out, Freddy!" she called. Then, almost imploringly, "Come out, Freddy, *please!*" She waited. At last she reached into

the cage and did what she had been tactful enough never to do before — she folded back the cover over my burrow. There was food inside (I eyed it sadly), but no Freddy.

"He's gone." She started to sob. It was heartbreaking for both of us, but unavoidable. Suddenly she raised her head. "The door was shut, I'm positive it was."

"Hmm . . ." Mr. John inspected the cage. All at once he bent forward. "What's that?" He pointed to my pencil, which was clearly visible. "How did that get in there?"

"Oh, that. It was a present from me. He wanted it."

161

"Is that so?" Mr. John rubbed his nose. "Perhaps he . . . Hmm . . . That would explain a couple of things."

"Like what?"

"Like certain changes to my bookshelves."

"I don't understand."

"Nor do I, to be honest, but there's a possibility Freddy opened the cage door by himself."

"By himself? How?"

"By using the pencil as a lever. It looks as if he's run away."

"Run away? You really think so?" Sophie looked over at her desk. "But where to?" She kneeled down on the floor and peered under the bed. "Where are you, Freddy?"

"Listen, kid." Mr. John squatted down beside her. "Whatever made him vanish, he's probably hiding someplace you can't find him. You'll only get him back if he *wants* to come back."

I really have to say this: The most sensible remarks I'd ever heard from any human being came from Mr. John.

"Here's a suggestion for you, Sophie." Mr. John

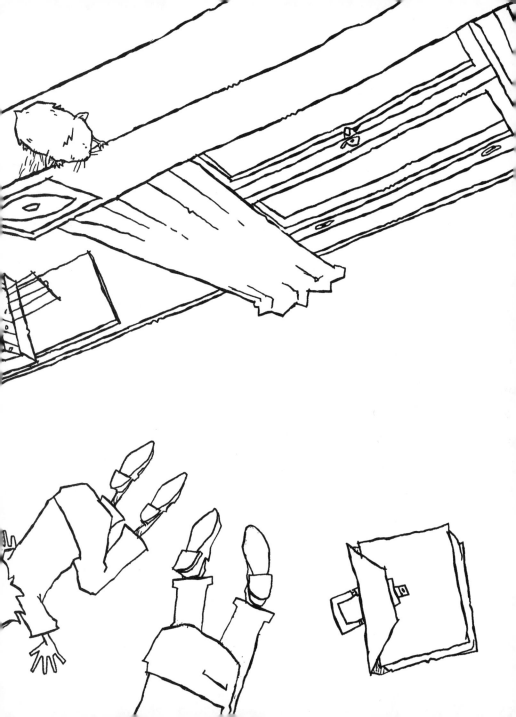

straightened up. "Put a couple of mealworms in his cage and we'll leave the room. We'll wait a while, then see if he's turned up again. Okay?"

Sophie nodded. She emptied a paper bag of mealworms (five of them, no less!) onto my feeding place and called, "Mealworms, Freddy!" That done, they both went out.

I gazed intently down from my hiding place, but not at the mealworms. They didn't interest me in the least, not now. I was interested in something altogether different — something lying on the floor, just where Mr. John had been squatting down — his leather briefcase.

At first I merely stared at the thing. It was lying on its side, not standing upright, which meant that the flap was on top and readily accessible from the floor. There was enough of a gap beneath it for a very small rodent to slip inside with ease. . . .

Suddenly I realized why I was staring so hard: The briefcase was my escape route, my passport to the outside world! I didn't have to stay here with Sophie, Gregory, and Mom. I could use Mr. John to take me back to his apartment. Once there, I could make up my own mind where to burrow.

If any of my readers think I clambered down the curtain without a second thought and disappeared into the briefcase like lightning, they're dead right. Some decisions are glaringly obvious.

The briefcase was divided into two compartments. As I crouched there amid an assortment of books with German titles (why on earth did the man tote them around all the time?), I regretted my decision a dozen times and applauded it a moment later. My doubts centered less on whether I ought to leave Sophie's home than on whether I would be welcome at Mr. John's. If Sir William didn't want me back, I might as well pack up and move on right away.

"I can hardly wait to see if he's there!" That was Sophie, outside in the hallway. The door opened, and I heard her and Mr. John come into the room.

There was silence for a moment. Then Mr. John said,

165

"Well, it seems he has other plans. To be on the safe side, leave the cage door open. Maybe he'll turn up after all. And now I have to go."

With all my might, I sank my teeth into the upper edge of the leather divider between the two compartments. I didn't want to be pitched off into the depths and crushed by books when Mr. John picked up his briefcase. But he righted it with care and picked it up quite gently.

"See you, kid," he said.

Good-bye, Sophie, I thought — forever, if I'm lucky.

Mr. John left the apartment and set off for home. It was the third time I had made that trip, twice in one direction and once in the other. The route was becoming central to my personal destiny.

Mr. John trudged up the steep flight of stairs to his apartment, opened the front door, and went into the study. If he put the briefcase on his desk, I would be at my wits' end once more. The only solution would be to get in touch with Sir William and ask him to lift me down in secret. But Mr. John deposited the briefcase on the floor.

Then his footsteps receded in the direction of the kitchen.
Nimble as a chipmunk, I squeezed through the gap, climbed
out, and slid to the floor. Where to now? Under the chest

of drawers in the corner. It was so near the ground that I felt safe there, at least for the moment.

This time, heaven knows, I was genuinely glad the air reeked of tomcat and guinea pig. The smell was like a breath of home.

"No, my friend, it's not as simple as that." Sir William regarded me with his glowing green eyes. It was evening now, and Mr. John had left the apartment to give a German lesson someplace. As for me, I had gone to report back, so to speak, to Sir William, who was waiting for me at the door to the living room.

"You come waltzing in here, planning to live in hiding." Sir William's eyeteeth glinted in the gloom. "How do you think you're going to manage for food?"

"Well," I said, "Enrico and Caruso get more than they need. I could —"

"You think they'll let you have some?"

"Yes, if you tell them to."

"My dear Freddy, do you imagine I only have to swish

my tail a couple of times for things to turn out the way I want? In this establishment, all decisions are communal decisions. Come with me."

We joined the guinea pigs in the room next door. They were sitting up and waiting for us in silence. They didn't embark on their performance until we were standing outside their cage — until their audience had settled down, so to speak.

"If it isn't good old Freddy!" cried Enrico. "He's back, by all that's holy! **WELL, I NEVER!**"

"Hurrah!" Caruso chimed in. "And we were both convinced he'd gone forever."

"But is he here our company to savor?"

"Or has he come to ask us for a favor?"

They had obviously overheard my conversation with Sir William.

Enrico sighed. "He'll need to find himself someplace to hide."

Caruso agreed, "Some nook or cranny? How undignified!"

169

"And where's his food to come from, what is more?"

"Let's share some with him. We've got food galore."

"Of course! We'll sit beside him, you and me —"

"— and offer him our hospitality."

Whereupon they broke into song:

"Great news! King Fred has granted our request

and kindly deigned to be our honored guest."

They had me at their mercy.

No doubt about it: Those jokers were serious. They wouldn't share a morsel of their food unless I sat down in their cage and played along with them.

IT WAS DO OR DIE.

Okay, but I had a few conditions first, and I intended to present them in a form that beat them at their own game. Surely I had become a better poet from all my nights of reading.

170

I drew myself up, but this time without overdoing it or blowing out my cheeks.

"It's true," I declared. "King Fred may possibly feel able
to take the place of honor at your table,
but only if your manners pass the test,
and what good manners are King Fred knows best."

Enrico and Caruso exchanged a glance. It must have
been dawning on them that they'd met their match.

"As king," I went on, "I make the rules, and I'm afraid
they must by all my subjects be obeyed.
First, thoroughly spring-clean your cage inside,
for scattered food I really can't abide.
The litter too, must always be kept dry,
for sodden straw offends the royal eye.
As for the food itself, last but not least,
King Fred on nothing but the best shall feast.
Obey these golden rules and, if you do,
His Majesty will deign to dine with you."

Silence.

Well, I thought, they'll find it hard to go along with that.

But what was that noise?

They were hooting with laughter — Enrico and Caruso were hugging each other and hooting with laughter. "He thinks he's put one over on us!" shrieked Enrico, and Caruso yelled, "He thinks: They're only guinea pigs, they can't help being the way they are!"

"He thinks we're incorrigible food-scatterers."

"And incorrigible litter-piddlers."

"Surprise, surprise!" they chanted in unison. "We're adaptable types. We can behave quite differently if we choose!"

"We condescend to grant your plea.
The two of us plus you makes three.
Feel free to join our gang, because
we welcome you with open paws.
You're now, although than us less big,
an honorary guinea pig."

"Well," Sir William said at length, "that seems to settle the food problem." He thought for a moment. "All the same," he went on, "you can't live in hiding here."

"But . . . why not?"

He stared at me in silence. Finally he said, "Because it would be wrong to go behind Mr. John's back."

It took a moment or two to sink in. Then I understood.

I Was Done For.

This was the end: I would have to go back to Sophie's place.

"I still think it's wrong, but there's only one solution that I can see." Sir William paused. "We'll have to get in touch with Mr. John after all."

CHaPTER SIXTEEN

TO GET THE NEW TYPEWRITER GOING and write
Mr. John a message, all I had to do was operate the start
button and press the correct series of keys — or so I
imagined. Sir William was hugely amused.

"My dear Freddy," he said with a smirk, "you may be an
expert on the written word, but not on a Mac — that's
what the new typewriter is called, by the way, a Mac computer. From what I've seen, you have to master a pretty
complicated procedure before you can start writing. I
suggest you study the instructions."

I did so the same evening, after Sir William had airlifted me onto the desk. I soon realized that it would be
two or three days before I was capable of using the Mac.
Which meant, unfortunately, that I would have to take
advantage of Enrico and Caruso's hospitality — and that
very night.

"But not until Mr. John's asleep in bed," decreed Sir

William, when he had jumped onto the desk to collect me. He jerked his head at the fat book with *User's Guide* on the cover. "Well, making any progress?"

I had already discovered that the thing resembling one of his paws was called a mouse. When I told him this, he smilingly remarked that mechanical mice didn't interest him — in fact he'd never even managed to acquire a taste for real ones. There was something he wanted to know, however. "You were eager to get in touch with Mr. John from the very first," he said. "Why? Where did you hope it would get you?"

"To the Promised Land of Assyria," I said.

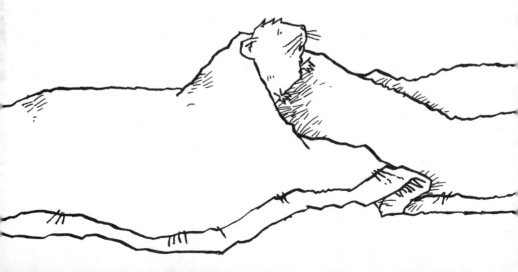

Sir William had settled down on his blanket, and I, to avoid being discovered too soon by Mr. John, was sitting under one of the folds near the edge. Sir William wanted to hear the whole story, so I recounted it from the very beginning. I told him about the cage in the pet shop; about Great-Grandmother and the Golden Hamster Saga; about the far-off Promised Land of Assyria, in which

Great-Grandmother herself did not believe too strongly; about the way I'd managed to attract a buyer; about my time with Sophie, Gregory, and Mom; about the way I'd learned to read; and last of all, about my escape in Mr. John's briefcase.

Then I told Sir William about my discovery. I said I'd gradually come to realize that Assyria was everywhere. It was not only outside your cage but inside it as well, in a burrow with well-stocked larders, first-class sports equipment, and the door left open at all times. It was wherever you wanted to be and could do whatever you wanted to do — like reading books, for example. For many a hamster, I said, Assyria could open up entirely new prospects. A hamster capable of writing might wind up in another, quite unprecedented kind of Assyria. On the other hand, you could do without all these things and still be in Assyria. "In short," I said, "a golden hamster in Assyria —"

"— is a civilized domestic animal free to roam wherever it wants," Sir William broke in.

I nodded, taken aback. I hadn't seen the matter in so

simple a light (a bit too simple, perhaps). "Anyway," I went on, "it's impossible to live like that without human co-operation. That's why I'm anxious to get in touch with Mr. John."

"Hmm," said Sir William. "And now you've almost attained your objective." He pondered awhile. "When you do, you can only hope for the best."

"MEANING WHAT?"

"My dear fellow, you belong to little Sophie. She wants you back. Mr. John may decide to return you to her."

My evening meal with Enrico and Caruso began on a pleasant note. The food strewn around their cage had been raked together into a neat little mound. They had even succeeded in rearranging their litter so that no damp patches could be seen (not that this had disposed of the smell problem, but the less said about that the better).

Sir William let me into the cage and then withdrew. Enrico and Caruso were decorously seated in front of a

179

small bowl that they had unearthed someplace and managed to clean. It was brimming with lettuce leaves and grain.

Enrico pointed to it, performing a kind of courtly bow as he did so:

> "As for the food itself, last but not least,
> King Fred on nothing but the best shall feast."

The words slipped out before I knew it:

> "His Majesty appreciates the care
> with which you've offered him such tasty fare."

Enrico and Caruso nodded, looking delighted. Caruso bowed too — surprisingly gracefully, in view of his fat tummy — and recited:

"We've gathered here tonight not just to dine,
but also intellectually to shine.
So let us doughty rhymesters boldly duel
and crown the victor with a wreath of laurel."

A poetry competition? Sorry, count me out. They'd gotten me far too deeply involved in their little game as it was.

"Listen," I said. "CUT OUT THE RHYMES, OKAY?"

Enrico and Caruso stared at me.

"I mean it, you guys. I came here to eat, not to make up poetry, you understand?"

They positively collapsed like burst balloons. It was a pitiful sight.

"Look," I said. "You made a great job of these preparations and you'd set your hearts on a poetry competition,

181

and now it's all come to nothing. It must be depressing, I know, but be honest: Can't you drop your little game for once? Can't you behave like serious individuals?"

They exchanged a look.

"We *could* be serious," Enrico said at length, "but we avoid it because — well, it makes life complicated, and we don't like complications."

"The truth is," Caruso confessed, staring at the floor, "being serious would give us a whole heap of things to brood about."

"Quite," said Enrico, restlessly shuffling to and fro. "We realized that this evening, when you were telling Sir William about Assyria."

"Exactly," Caruso blurted out. "As I said to my friend here, 'Where is *our* Assyria, Enrico?'"

"Yes, why are we shut up in here?" Enrico demanded in a trembling voice. "Why can't *we* be civilized domestic animals free to roam wherever we want?"

"We're clean enough, aren't we?" Caruso gestured at the cage, then clamped a paw over his eyes. "We may smell

a bit strong," he sobbed, his shoulders shaking, "but that we can't help." He began to weep in earnest.

I hadn't known that guinea pigs could weep.

But Caruso was definitely weeping.

Enrico's shoulders too, were shaking. "We're rodents like any others," he sobbed. "Why do people despise us so?"

And they wept and whimpered in unison.

Gee . . . I sat there looking at them feeling utterly helpless. Who would have thought them capable of such mental anguish? I felt a lump gather in my throat.

I hemmed and hawed a couple of times. "Now listen, you guys . . ."

Their sobbing intensified.

Or rather, it underwent a change. The sobs became gurgles, grew louder still, turned into splutters, and suddenly exploded into a barrage of hoots, shrieks, and guffaws. Enrico and Caruso were bellowing with mirth. They reached out and hugged each other, rocking to and fro with laughter.

I could have bitten Enrico in the neck, driven my teeth into Caruso's plump butt. I could have torn them to shreds!

Get out of here, I commanded myself. Don't blow a fuse, take it easy, stay cool, just calmly exit the cage.

Luckily, Sir William had left the door open. Enrico and Caruso were still hooting with laughter, quite unaware of their narrow escape. I had already reached the cage door when I remembered why I'd come. Should I? Of course. I'd fulfilled their conditions, so I had every right to.

184

I turned around, went calmly over to the bowl of food, and swiftly — but far from hurriedly — filled my cheek pouches.

Enrico and Caruso had stopped laughing and were darting glances at me. Some guardian angel prompted them to keep their mouths shut, but it was obvious they wouldn't be able to restrain themselves for long. Sure

185

enough, just as I was climbing out of the cage with my cheek pouches full to bursting, they were off again:

"All day long we sing our song
and whistle as we do so.
No guinea pigs sing better than
Enrico and Caruso.

A hamster doesn't sing, it squeaks
and stuffs its cheeks with fodder
until they swell up like balloons.
No creature could look odder. . . ."

I found myself rhyming without meaning to:

"Yes, yes, you guys, I've heard that one before.
Your dumb song doesn't rile me anymore."

*　*　*

Having stowed my food under the chest of drawers in the study, I remained in hiding for the next few days. All I could see from there, unfortunately, were Mr. John's shoes, so I couldn't actually watch him writing. He spent all day at his desk, and I could hear the faint click the keys of the new typewriter made when he pressed them down. (A hamster's sensitive ears find the invention of the computer a real blessing.)

Sophie came to visit one afternoon.

"Hi, kid," said Mr. John. "Has Freddy turned up yet?"

"No," she said sadly. "Daddy says he may never come back. That's because we live in such an old building. There are too many hiding places."

"How about your mom? Has she had that allergy again?"

Sophie must have shaken her head, because she went on, "But if she does, she says we'll have to set some traps."

Just as I had feared. I could thank my lucky stars I'd managed to escape in the nick of time.

"Daddy says I can have another golden hamster, but I don't want one. I'm absolutely positive Freddy will turn up again."

"What if he doesn't? How do we know what his plans are? He's gone for the time being, that's for sure."

But not for much longer. Whether I remained here or was compelled to go back to Sophie's place, my uncertainty had to be dispelled. The stress was reducing my life expectancy. I decided to leave Mr. John a message that very evening.

"What do you plan to say?" asked Sir William.

"I don't quite know yet," I replied nervously, turning over another page in the User's Guide.

Evening had come at last. Mr. John had left the apartment and I had set to work. Sir William requested to stay and watch. I could hardly object, especially as he had airlifted me onto the desk. If he thought I would let him dictate my message to Mr. John, however, he was very much mistaken.

"I'm not asking because I want to dictate to you in any way," Sir William said, "only to advise you on how to word your message. After all, I've known Mr. John a good bit longer than you."

"Thanks," I said, feeling somewhat ashamed, "but the wording of the message isn't the real problem."

"So what is?"

"Everything else." I sighed. All I actually knew was how to turn on the Mac. I could only guess at what I had to do before I started typing, but that I would discover by trial and error — the User's Guide gave one or two hints on the subject. "The real problem is, how will Mr. John get to know about the message?"

"By reading it?" hazarded Sir William.

"He'll have to see it first," I said with a pitying smile. My feline friend was getting rather old and slow on the uptake, I reflected. "I want the message to appear on the screen as soon as he switches on the Mac. I don't know how to fix that, but there must be a way. It says something about it in —"

"Freddy?"

"— in the User's Guide. Yes, what is it?"

"My dear Freddy, we can simply leave the Mac on."

I stared at him.

"I'm right, aren't I?" said Sir William. "Then he'll find the message waiting for him when he comes home."

At that moment I felt more than somewhat ashamed.

"Don't take it to heart." Sir William grinned. "Experts often fail to see the forest for the trees." He paused. "Well, any other problems?"

"Just a teensy one. What if Mr. John doesn't believe it?"

"You mean, what if he doesn't believe that the message came from you? That there's something wrong with the Mac? That it produced the message by accident, or something?"

I nodded.

"My dear Freddy, allow me to tell you a few things about Mr. John." Sir William was clearly preparing to deliver a lengthy lecture, but he restrained himself in time. "Well, I'll tell you this much," he said. "Nothing ever shakes him. He's inquisitive too. If a golden hamster writes to him out of the blue, he won't say to himself, 'This can't be true. If it is, my world has gone haywire and I've lost my marbles.' He'll say, 'Well, well, how interesting!'" Sir William paused. Then he added, "Not, of course, that it would prevent him from taking you back to Sophie."

Quite. That question would be settled in the near future, and that was what I was afraid of — mightily afraid of.

"There's only one way to find out," said Sir William.

I nodded.

Okay. Go, Freddy, go.

Write your message.

I went over to the right-hand side of the keyboard and raised my paw. Sir William gave me a nod, and I brought it down on the start button.

The gong sounded; the Mac began to hum.

After a while the screen displayed a series of symbols. Although I already knew what some of them meant, most were alarmingly unfamiliar.

Then the image on the screen came to rest. It looked like the picture in the User's Guide. The Mac was now switched on and ready for use. I could go ahead and write my message to Mr. John.

But what was that?

The image on the screen had started changing again. Symbols appeared and disappeared. Then the image steadied once more.

The screen was now white, and some black letters had appeared on its blank surface.

The letters formed words. Something was already written on the screen.

I read:

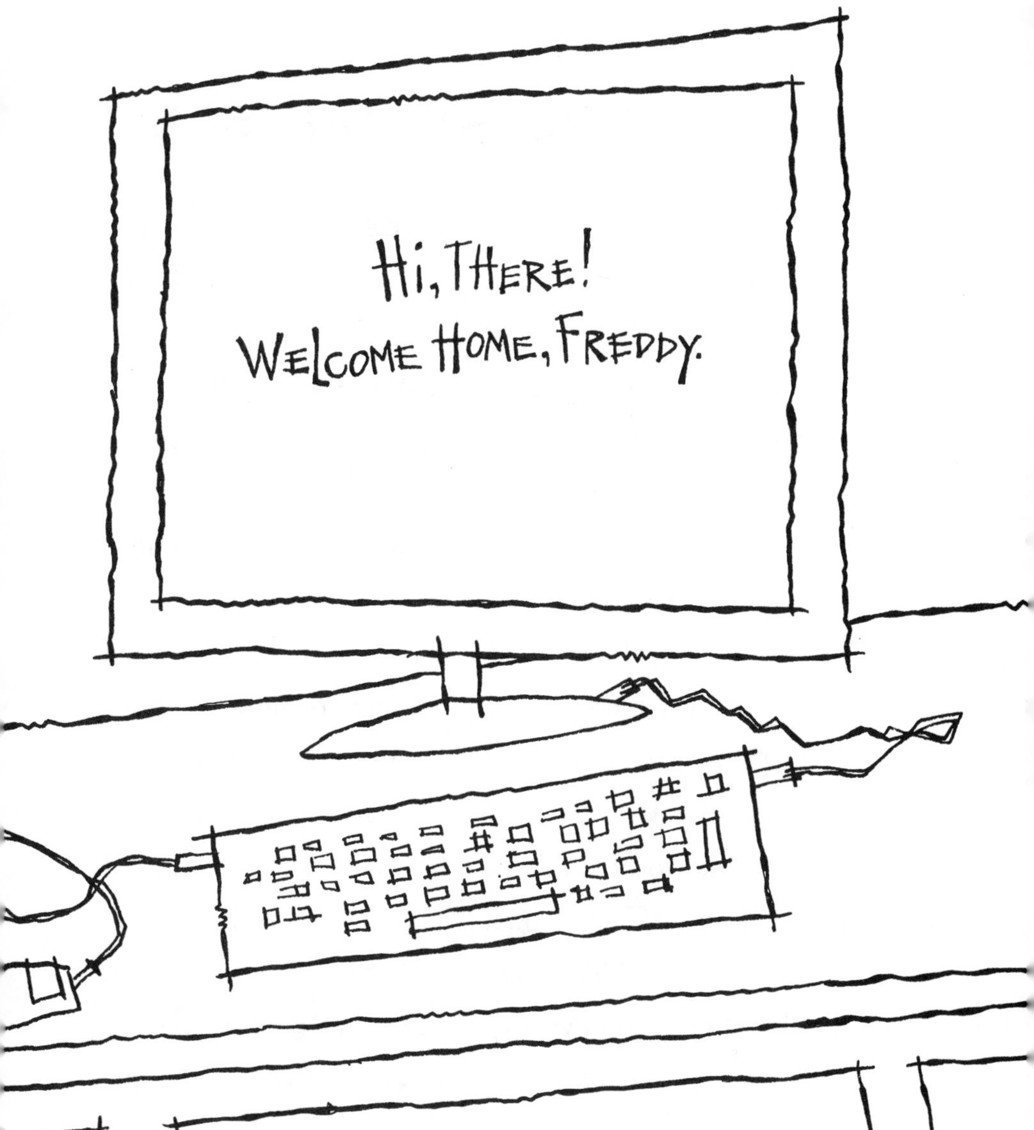
Hi, THERE!
WELCOME HOME, FREDDY.

CHaPTER SEVENTEEN

MY CAGE — OR RATHER, MY RESIDENCE (the door remains open at all times) — is back in its place on the third shelf up. Mr. John has taken my advice and tacked a strip of net curtain to the top shelf. It extends all the way to the floor. Another strip is suspended from the edge of the desk, so I don't have to ask Sir William to jump up there anymore. In any case, he considers such exertions unsuitable at his age.

The door of Enrico and Caruso's cage is always open too, by the way, but they're seldom seen roaming the apartment. They prefer to stay home, they say, and continue their theatrical training. They also requested Mr. John, through me, to be kind enough to adjust the position of their cage so as to give them a better view of the TV set.

So far, Sir William has steadfastly refused to get in touch with Mr. John via the Mac. He just goes on purring and meowing at him, but that way he'll never get the infrared lamp he covets to warm his fur with. Personally, I shall take care not to interfere in any way. Sir William can get very huffy when he thinks he's being bullied into something. He and I have been the best of friends ever since I grasped that fact.

We've only had one major spat, and that was the night I first got in touch with Mr. John.

Having more or less deciphered his message of welcome, I proceeded to draft a reply. It had to be brief and to the point, so this is what I came up with:

Thanks for giving me houseroom, Mr. John.

Sir William objected to this wording. It wouldn't do, he said — it was disrespectful.

At first I couldn't fathom what he meant. Then it turned out that he thought it would be more appropriate for me to address Mr. John as "Master." I argued that to call someone "Master" implied that he owned me, and no self-respecting animal could admit to being owned like a piece of furniture.

I found Sir William's attitude absurd and told him so.

This made him rather angry. He continued to raise objections, which only made me dig in my heels — he *was* trying to dictate to me after all! To make a long story short, I came close to squandering my opportunity. This dawned on me at a lucid moment, so I suggested the following alternative:

Dear Mr. John, many thanks for allowing me to live in your home as a civilized hamster free to roam wherever he wants.

Sir William found this an excellent solution. That not only settled our dispute but gave me somewhat more of an insight into the way the old gentleman's mind worked.

It was a considerable time before I managed to get my message down on the screen. After that, I proposed simply to wait, sitting on the desk, for Mr. John to come home. Sir William pronounced this extremely unwise. He said I should give "the Master" time to get used to the new situation and think about things — for instance, how to inform little Sophie that her beloved Freddy would be living with him from now on. He was right, so I spent the night under the chest of drawers.

In fact, Mr. John's only response when he found my message on the screen was "Hmm . . ." Then he switched off the Mac and retired to bed without further comment.

The next morning he called my name. I came out from under the chest of drawers. Presumably taking my consent for granted, he picked me up and deposited me on the desk beside the Mac, which was already switched on.

"Listen, kid," he said, "there's something we must straighten out. If you agree with

what I say, press the Y key; if not, press the N. If you want something explained in greater detail, press M for 'more.' Right?"

I pressed the Y key.

Then he told me we couldn't avoid letting Sophie know about my reappearance, even at the risk of her wanting me back. I needn't be afraid, though; he would talk her into letting me stay. I pressed the M key.

He had a translation to complete and was rather pressed for time, he said, so I would simply have to trust him. I thought awhile, then pressed the Y.

"Next point," said Mr. John. "The fact that you can read and write must remain a secret between us."

I pressed the M, then an exclamation mark.

"Why?" he said. "Because, with all due respect to Sophie

and her parents, if the three of them knew about your unique talents, it's pretty certain other people would get to know too. Sophie would only have to open her mouth in school one day. And then what? It wouldn't be long before some smart showman came along, eager to make a fortune out of Fantastic Freddy, the hamster that can read and write. Either that, or you'd wind up in the hands of scientists itching to dissect your brain for research purposes. Does either of those prospects appeal to you?"

I pressed the N key several times.

"So it's a deal: strict secrecy. Now I'll have a word with Sophie."

He picked up the phone.

"Hello, kid. Freddy's turned up. . . . Yes, here in my apartment. . . . No, no, hold your horses, first let me . . . How? He hid in my briefcase. Listen, kid, you must have a pretty good idea of why he ran away. . . . The cage door? He opened it with your pencil — got hold of it on purpose, as I suspected. . . . Yes, very smart of him, I agree. . . . Hmm . . . But here he could have the run of the place. . . . No, William would never hurt him, I know it for a fact. . . . Yes, I think so too. Freddy definitely needs his freedom. . . . Okay, that's settled, then. See you soon."

He hung up and turned to me. "Well, Freddy . . ." He broke off and smiled. The screen was now displaying the words:

Thanks for everything, Mr. John.

It wasn't long before Sophie turned up with Gregory, who had brought my cage along. When they came into the room I was still sitting on the desk beside the Mac (the screen was now as blank as a sheet of white paper). I sat up and waved.

Gregory laughed. "That's how he got me to buy him, the rascal."

"Freddy isn't a rascal," said Sophie. "He's the bestest, smartest golden hamster in the world."

You don't know how right you are, Sophie.

"Here, Freddy." She put a mealworm in front of me. "You're staying with Mr. John because you're better off here. But I'll come and visit you, okay?"

Okay, Sophie. Sorry I can't give you that in writing, but unfortunately the fact that I can write must remain a secret.

The poem!

A mighty pain to love it is,
and 'tis a pain that pain to miss;
but of all pains the greatest pain
it is to love, but love in vain.

I'd picked it out for her specially. Now I would never be able to show it to her. I was doubly sorry.

But still, I really couldn't complain. I might not be able to write to Sophie, but now I could write to my heart's content.

I made a start the very next day. To begin with, I limited myself to finger exercises — paw exercises, I mean — on the Mac's keyboard. Before long, however, I could manipulate the keys so skillfully that I was able to type my messages to Mr. John on the screen without difficulty. As time went by I developed an urge to write something really long, but not just any old thing. I wanted to write a story — a regular story like the ones in the books on Mr. John's shelves. That was a tall order. On the other hand, I knew exactly what my story would be about.

And then, one evening, the moment came.

Enrico and Caruso had settled down at last, Sir William had retired to his blanket for the night, and Mr. John had gone out.

Suddenly, I knew it: Now was the time to start writing my life story.

The story of a golden hamster who set off in search of the Promised Land of Assyria.

CHAPTER ONE

The time has come.

Enrico and Caruso, the guinea pigs, have settled down at last, old William the tomcat has retired to his blanket for the night, and Mr. John has gone out.

Now is the time to make a start on my life story. . . .

DIETLOF REICHE grew up in a family of five children. Over the years, the family adopted seven hamsters, but unfortunately, they eventually all ran away. Dietlof always wondered why they left and where they went. So he imagined Freddy, and there began the Golden Hamster Saga. Dietlof Reiche lives in Hamburg, Germany, with his wife.

JOHN BROWNJOHN has translated over one hundred books for children and adults. He lives in England.

JOE CEPEDA has created artwork for numerous book covers, magazines, and newspapers. He is also the illustrator of many award-winning picture books. He lives in California with his family.

FOLLOW FREDDY'S FURTHER ADVENTURES!

FREDDY IN PERIL
BOOK TWO
IN THE GOLDEN HAMSTER SAGA

and

FREDDY TO THE RESCUE
BOOK THREE
IN THE GOLDEN HAMSTER SAGA